The Orphan's Lost Hope

©2023 by Molly Britton

All rights reserved. No part of this may be reproduced, distributed or transmitted in any form or by any means without prior written permission.
These stories are works of fiction. Names, characters, places and incidents are the product of the author's imagination and are used fictitiously. Any resemblance to events, locales or actual persons, living or dead, is entirely coincidental.

Contents

Chapter 1

Chapter 2

Chapter 3

Chapter 4

Chapter 5

Chapter 6

Chapter 7

Chapter 8

Chapter 9

Chapter 10

Chapter 11

Chapter 12

Chapter 13

Epilogue

Chapter 1

The rain poured down relentlessly as Nora and Sally trudged through the muddy streets of London, their thin clothes soaked through and their teeth chattering from the cold. The city was a harsh place for the poor, and the sisters knew this better than most.

Nora, who was eight, and her younger sister, Sally, who was six, had just lost their parents to cholera. They were a loving family who lived in a small, run-down house on the outskirts of the city. But when the disease hit, it took their parents quickly, leaving Nora and Sally alone in the world.

The girls had no family to take them in, so they were sent to the workhouse, which was a place where the poor and desperate had to live and work to survive.

"Nora, I'm tired," Sally whimpered in a small, weak voice.

"I know, Sal," said Nora in the same soft tone. "Soon we'll be there."

Nora's stomach churned with fear as she approached the dark, imposing workhouse. She had heard horrible things about what happened inside its walls. But there was nothing else she could do. They had no other choice.

Upon entering the dreary building, Nora's mood plummeted even further. The space was insufficient to accommodate the excessive number of people crammed inside, and the odour of sickness and deterioration pervaded the entire place. The girls were confined in a spacious room with numerous other children, some of whom were weeping or coughing.

A gruff woman with a stern face came over to them, eyeing them up and down. "Names?"

"Nora and Sally Lewis," Nora replied, trying to sound brave.

The woman scribbled their names down on a clipboard before gesturing towards a corner of the room. "You two can sleep over there."

Nora and Sally made their way to the designated area, where a few thin mattresses lay on the floor. Nora helped Sally get settled in before curling up next to her, pulling a thin blanket over their shivering bodies.

As they lay there, listening to the sounds of coughing and moaning all around them, Sally started to cry. "I miss Mum and Dad," she whimpered.

Nora held her sister close, her own eyes filling with tears. "I know, Sal. I miss them too. But we have to be strong. We'll get through this together."

The next morning, the two girls were roused from their sleep at an early hour and were put to work in the laundry room. Nora was given a large basket full of soiled garments to wash, and she began scrubbing away at them with an intense focus. Meanwhile, Sally was instructed to fold the newly washed clothes, but she found the task to be challenging and struggled to keep up with the pace.

Observing her sister's difficulty, Nora grew concerned, realizing that if Sally didn't catch up, they would both be punished. "Come on, Sal," she encouraged her sibling while taking some of her clothes to fold. "Let me help you."

Throughout the day, they labored without respite, pushing themselves to their limits. By the time evening arrived, they were both exhausted and famished. Nora fed Sally what little they had remaining of their meager food before tucking her into bed.

"We'll find a way out of this place, Sal," Nora whispered to her sister, her own stomach rumbling. "I promise."

Determined to keep her sister secure and escape from the workhouse, Nora's perseverance only grew stronger. She was aware that the road ahead would be arduous and lengthy, but she was prepared to do whatever it took to keep Sally safe and regain their freedom.

***

Nora and Sally soon discovered that life at the workhouse would be far from easy. They had to make do with shabby clothes, a single bed, and a meagre diet of gruel and bread. The workload was heavy, and the living conditions were less than ideal.

Despite Nora's best efforts to keep Sally safe and healthy, it was a challenge. The younger child's weak immune system made her prone to frequent colds and coughs.

Whenever Sally felt scared or upset, Nora would wrap her in extra blankets, offer her a cup of hot tea, and comfort her with kind words.

The limited ties the girls established with other children at the workhouse provided them with some relief. Emma, the oldest of her three siblings, liked Nora and Sally. Emma, who was only a couple of years older than Nora, constantly kept an eye on her younger sisters.

Emma strolled over to the girls as they were doing laundry one day, smiling slightly. She held up a badly made wooden horse and said, "I have something for you. It was crafted for you by my younger brother. He believes that you are the bravest females in the workhouse."

Nora's heart swelled with gratitude. Though it was a small gesture, it meant the world to her and Sally. She took the horse and thanked Emma, promising to keep it safe.

As the days turned into weeks, Nora continued to look out for Sally and forge connections with the other children. But she knew that if they wanted a chance at a better life, they would have to find a way out of the workhouse. It would take resourcefulness, ingenuity, and determination, but Nora was willing to do whatever it took to ensure that she and Sally never had to endure such hardship again.

Every day was full of exhausting work, strict rules, and minimal rations. The girls were given meagre portions of cheese or fruit, if any at all, with their porridge and bread. If

Sally didn't have enough to eat, Nora would sacrifice her own food to make sure her sister was fed.

Nora overheard a conversation between two older girls while sweeping the floor of the laundry room. One of them replied, "I've heard there's a way out of this place."

"That may not work, however. It demands courage and cleverness to accomplish."

Nora approached the girls and questioned about what they were discussing. One of the older girls, Mary, advised her that a tunnel might be used to escape the building. A gang of older boys discovered it years ago, but once they were caught and punished, no one else attempted it.

Nora could not stop considering the possibility of underground escape. She could no longer tolerate the idea of Sally being mistreated or punished, yet attempting to flee carried a serious cost. She cautioned Mary that travelling alone was risky.

Mary shrugged and responded, "It's up to you, but let me know if you change your mind."

All day, Nora could not get the thought from her mind. Could they escape via the tunnel? The idea of freedom and a better life was too alluring to reject. She needed to conduct further research.

Nora asked her sister, "Sally, do you want to leave this place?" as they laid in bed together that night.

Sally eagerly agreed. "Yes, Nora. I hate it here."

Nora told her there was a chance they could escape, but it was risky and they could be caught and punished. She promised Sally that she would be safe if they tried.

Over the next few days, Nora and Sally researched the tunnel and gathered information. They talked to older children in the neighbourhood, listened in on conversations, and kept an eye out for anything unusual. Nora also observed the daily routines of the workhouse staff to identify any potential opportunities.

In the midst of a dark and stormy night, Nora and Sally snuck to the basement and discovered the tunnel's entrance. It was dark, wet, and unpleasant, yet they persisted.

They had been in the tunnel for what seemed like hours before emerging into a tiny chamber. The slats of an open door allowed Nora to see a glimmer of light. She warily approached, listening for any indications of danger. She believed that she had heard distant footsteps. She opened the door gradually and peered outside.

Despite the torrential downpour, they were ultimately liberated. They stumbled onto a tiny lane behind the workhouse. Nora stretched out and grabbed Sally's hand, happy that they had successfully escaped the building.

Nora and Sally fled as quickly as they could in an effort to get as far away from the workhouse as possible. The rain continued to pour down, wetting them both to the bone. Yet they cared not; they were free.

Nora led the way down the meandering streets, her eyes darting back and forth, seeking for any indication of danger. Sally staggered behind Nora, her little fingers firmly gripping Nora's.

"Where do we intend to go, Nora?" Sally's voice was barely audible over the sound of the rain as she questioned.

Nora said, "I don't know yet," as she scanned the area for any cover they may seek. "But we cannot remain in this exposed location. We need to locate somewhere to hide."

They turned a corner and noticed a little alleyway up ahead. Nora hastily pushed Sally along, squeezing into the tight area between two buildings. They snuggled together in an attempt to be as dry as possible.

"We made it, Sal," Nora muttered. "We are free."

Sally's face lit up with a smile, which vanished as soon as she looked up at Nora. "What are our next steps?"

Nora exhaled as her mind raced with ideas and plans. "We must find a place to spend the night. Thereafter, we will determine our future moves."

They shivered and were soaked for what seemed like hours until the rain stopped. Nora's heart sunk as they exited the alley. They were still in the same drab area of town, surrounded by decrepit buildings and untidy streets.

Nora asserted resolutely, "We cannot stay here; we need to find a way out of this section of town."

They travelled for what seemed like miles in search of a spot to rest. Yet every inn and boarding house they came across was either too pricey or too crowded. Nora was beginning to lose hope when they discovered a little park.

"We can spend the night here," she remarked as she led Sally to a little seat beneath a tree. Although it is not much, it is better than nothing."

They used their lightweight clothing as makeshift blankets and huddled close. Sally fell asleep within minutes, but Nora stayed awake, her mind racing with ideas and concerns.

The following morning, they awoke to the sound of birds singing and light pouring down upon them. A surge of relaxation filled Nora, causing her to stretch. They had endured their first night on the run successfully.

She mumbled as she studied the park, "We need to get food. We must then determine our next steps."

As they travelled through the city, Nora kept a cautious look out for any signals of danger. Nora knew they couldn't stop to relax as they walked through packed marketplaces and busy streets, yet she couldn't help but smile. They had to continue travelling.

A bunch of men suddenly emerged around the corner and blocked their passage. Nora's pulse pounded as she sought a means of escape, but it was too late.

"Well, well, well," one of the men said with a sneer. "What do we have here?"

Nora tightened her grasp on Sally's hand, attempting to block the men's view of her younger sister. "Please," she pleaded in a trembling voice. "We don't want any difficulty."

The men chuckled, moving closer. Nora could smell the odour of alcohol on their breath.

"Sorry, sweetheart," another man remarked. "Yet, you two appear to be of some value to us."

They surged forward, grasping onto Nora and Sally's arms. Nora fought back with every ounce of her power, but she was no match for the raw force of the guys.

Chapter 2

The men who had captured Nora and Sally carried them back to the workhouse despite their pleadings for compassion. Nora attempted to fight back, but her might was no match for theirs. Sally was too weak to put up much of a fight, so she clutched Nora's hand as they were brought back to the location from which they had attempted to flee.

As they returned to the workhouse, the headmaster awaited their arrival. He was a vicious man with a severe appearance and a short fuse. He reprimanded Nora and Sally for their escape and warned them that they would be severely punished for their disobedience.

The penalty was severe. Nora and Sally were forced to spend hours washing and drying clothing in the laundry room. They were provided with considerably less food than previously, and they were forced to sleep on the ground without a bed.

Nora, despite their dire circumstances, refused to surrender. She continued to protect and care for Sally, and she made friends with other youngsters living in the workhouse. They discussed their hopes for a better life, of escaping the workhouse and beginning over.

Tom constituted one of Nora's closest companions. He was a few years older than Nora and had spent the majority of his life in the workhouse. When the workhouse rations were particularly poor, he instructed Nora on how to pick pockets and steal food.

Nora disliked stealing, but she knew that it was the only way to live at the workhouse. She tried to be as careful as possible, constantly making sure that she and Sally wouldn't get caught. Yet, one day they were.

Nora and Sally had just left the laundry room with stolen bread when they heard a yell from behind. They turned around to find the headmaster and two of his assistants racing towards them. Nora attempted to sprint, but her exhausted legs wouldn't comply.

The headmaster grabbed her forcibly by the arm, and his aides removed Sally from the room. Nora fought back, but the three of them were superior. They hauled her back to the workhouse, where she was shoved into a tiny, dark cell and left there to rot.

Nora was frightened. She had heard tales of the "black hole," a punishment chamber where children were held without food or drink for days. She didn't know how long she would be there, or whether she would ever see Sally again.

Nora's appetite and thirst grew as the days passed. She attempted to sleep, but the uncomfortable ground prohibited her from doing so. She deeply missed Sally and was anxious for her health. But, she did not give up. She was determined to survive regardless of the odds.

After what felt like an eternity, the door of the cell squeaked open. Nora's eyes adjusted to the unexpectedly bright light by blinking. She saw the administrator standing there with a sneering expression.

"Oh, well, well," he said. "See who's awake at last! You have been there for three days, as you are aware. Three days without water or food. I hope you've learnt your lesson."

Nora didn't say anything. She simply gazed at him with contempt in her eyes.

The administrator moved forward. "Your younger sister Sally is safe and well. Yet, if you continue to behave in this manner, she won't be for long. It's lucky that I'm in a giving mood today. You may leave at any time. Remember, Nora, if you try to escape a second time, the punishment will be more severe."

Nora exited from her cell in a fog, very tired. Her mind was a whirlpool of anger and annoyance. She could not believe how close they had come to freedom before being recaptured and sent back to the workhouse. She recognised that, in the future, they would have to be more cautious if they intended to escape for good.

Nora could hear the other youngsters whispering and giggling behind her back as she made her way back to the dormitory. She knew that they had seen her being carried away by the administrator, and now they were undoubtedly whispering about her and Sally. Nora attempted to ignore them and keep her head down, but it was impossible to filter out the sound of their vicious laughing.

When she eventually entered the dormitory, Nora found Sally curled up on her bed, looking pale and exhausted. Nora sat down next to her and grasped her hand. "Are you okay, Sally?" she kindly inquired.

Sally nodded faintly. "I'm okay, Nora. But I'm hungry. Do you have any food?"

Nora exhaled. Since their arrival in the workhouse, they had been given very little food, and Nora was compelled to give most of what they had to Sally so that she could maintain her vitality. She vowed, "I'll examine my options."

Nora got up and proceeded to the dormitory's entrance. She was resolved to obtain some of the matron's food supply, which she knew was kept in her office. Nora walked down the dark corridor and knocked on the door of the matron.

After a little interval, the door squeaked open. The matron stood at the doorway, staring down her nose at Nora. "What do you want?" she said coldly.

Nora took a deep breath and attempted to maintain a calm voice. "My sister and I are quite hungry. May we have some food?"

The matron regarded Nora for a time before letting out a brief, humourless chuckle. "Food? You believe I have extra food? You need to be thankful for what you have, daughter."

Nora's heart fell. She was aware that debating with the matron was impossible. She felt disappointed as she turned and headed back to the dormitory.

As Sally returned to the hostel, she saw Sally sitting up in bed, looking concerned. "Have you eaten, Nora?" she inquired.

Nora gave a headshake. "I apologise, Sally. The matron refused to provide us any."

Sally's face dropped. She muttered, "But I'm starving!"

Nora felt a twinge of remorse. She was aware that she needed to assist Sally. She scanned the room in quest for inspiration. Then she noticed it: a little window near the dormitory's ceiling.

Nora approached the window and looked up. She believed that she might be able to fit through it if she attempted it.

"I have an idea," she whispered to Sally. "But, you must pledge to keep quiet and stay still."

Sally nodded, appearing both terrified and fascinated.

Nora inhaled deeply and then climbed onto one of the mattresses. She reached up and gripped the window's edge, then pulled herself up until her head was level with the window. She cautiously scanned the area to ensure that no one was looking before attempting to squeeze through the window.

Nora had to contort her body to squeeze through the small doorway. It took a bit of effort, but eventually she managed to wriggle through and found herself on the roof of the workhouse.

Nora was caught off guard by the enormity of the workhouse when she glanced down from above. As she looked ahead, she observed a long series of windows and realised she needed to be cautious to avoid being seen. She started thinking about how she could get down to the ground level and get some food for Sally.

After a few minutes of searching, Nora discovered a small roof opening that led to a storage room. She entered the room with care and immediately began searching for food. She discovered some stale bread and potatoes, which she wrapped in a cloth and carried back to the roof.

Nora sneaked back into the dormitory where Sally was sleeping with the food in her possession. She gently awoke her sister and fed her the meagre meal. Sally ate slowly, savouring each bite, and Nora felt gratified that she was able to provide for her sister.

Nora continued to sneak out of the dormitory at night to find food for Sally over the following weeks. It was dangerous, and she constantly feared being caught, but she was determined to keep her sister alive.

As the days turned into weeks, Nora grew increasingly exhausted. She was getting little rest, and the stress of constantly sneaking around was taking its toll. She was aware that she could not continue indefinitely.

While Nora and Sally were working in the laundry room one day, they heard a disturbance outside. They peered through the window and observed a group of men in suits approaching the workhouse. Nora recognised them as Poor Law Board representatives.

As soon as Nora realised they would be inspected, she was overcome with fear. If they were caught with the food Nora had stolen, they would be severely punished. She quickly warned Sally to be quiet and attempted to conceal the food beneath dirty laundry.

The men entered the room and began inspecting the workhouse. Nora held her breath as they passed, fervently hoping they would not notice the food.

One of the officials, however, discovered the cloth Nora had used to wrap the bread and potatoes. He picked it up and removed the wrapping to expose the food inside.

He demanded, "What is this?" before turning to Nora.

Nora froze, unable to speak. She was aware that they were in peril.

The official went on. "Food theft is a serious crime, young lady. You will be punished for your actions."

While Nora thought of Sally, tears stung her eyes. She'd failed to safeguard her sister again.

Unexpectedly, one of the other officials then spoke up. "Wait a minute," he said, "This girl has been attempting to care for her younger sister. Consider how thin and ill she is. Perhaps we should be assisting them rather than punishing them."

The chief official hesitated briefly before nodding in agreement. "Very well," he said. "We'll overlook this for now. However, know that we will be monitoring your behaviour."

The officials then exited the room, and Nora collapsed to the ground in relief. She was appreciative of the leniency, but she was aware that they were still in a perilous situation. They would need to be even more cautious going forward.

As they returned to their jobs, Nora became increasingly determined to leave the workhouse. Her continual terror and struggle for existence had become unbearable. She felt she had to find a way to enhance Sally's life as well as her own.

Nora became more acquainted with the workhouse duties as the days went by. She observed the other youngsters and adults working nonstop from daylight to night, scarcely pausing to rest or eat. The work was difficult and risky, and Nora witnessed numerous injuries and accidents.

Despite the workhouse's gloomy and hopeless atmosphere, Nora refused to give up. She was dead set on escaping and taking Sally with her. She knew they needed to be cautious and patient, waiting for the proper moment to strike.

Nora also continued to look out for Sally, bringing her additional food scraps whenever she could find them and making sure she was warm and safe. Sally's health gradually improved, and she regained some of her strength and energy.

Yet Nora also had to deal with other difficulties. One of the older lads at the workhouse, a bully named Curt, developed a disliking for Nora and began harassing her and Sally whenever he could. Nora attempted to stay as far away from him as possible, but he seemed to be everywhere, lurking around corners and looking for trouble.

When Nora was out gathering firewood one day, Curt cornered Sally and began tormenting her. Nora heard her sister's calls for help and hurried as fast as she could back to the workhouse. When she arrived, she discovered Curt squeezing Sally's arm painfully.

Nora made no hesitation. She charged towards Curt, yelling at him to let go of Sally.

Curt snarled and pushed Sally to the ground before turning to confront Nora.

"What are you going to do, little girl?" he scoffed.

Nora remained silent. She pounced at Curt and threw him to the ground. Sally stared in terror as they tumbled around punching and kicking each other.

Nora eventually gained the upper hand, putting Curt on the ground with her knees on his chest. She looked down at him, her breathing heavy.

"Do you hear me when I say you leave us alone?" she yelled. "Or else," she added.

Curt only yelled at her and attempted to release himself. But Nora didn't give up, pinning him down until he gave up and slunk away, cursing under his breath.

After that incident, Curt mostly left Nora and Sally alone. Yet Nora knew he was still out there, looking for another opportunity to wreak trouble.

In spite of numerous challenges, Nora was determined not to give up hope. She was resolved to escape the workhouse and begin a new life with Sally in a place where they could live freely and happily. For the time being, though, they had to deal with each day as it came and rely on one another for strength and support.

Chapter 3

Sadness filled Nora's heart when she awoke early. She had been dreading the day she had to say goodbye to her sister Sally, and now that day had finally come. Since their parents' death, Nora and her sister had remained inseparable. Nora turned thirteen this year.

Nora had been summoned to the Matron's office the night prior. Nora was worried, unsure if they had done the right thing. But, the Matron had told her that the titled Lady Alva Colby was on the hunt for a maid. It had been decided that Nora would serve as a maid in the home of Lady Alva.

At hearing this, Nora felt a crushing sadness. That she would have to abandon Sally was a reality she had to face. At age eleven, Sally was too young to be a maid. Nora was unsure of her ability to handle life without her now that she was confined to the workhouse.

Nora gathered her few possessions into a bag and left the next morning. With tears running down her cheeks, she hugged Sally passionately. "Don't worry. As soon as I can, I'll be back for you."

Sally frantically held on to Nora. "I'm going to miss you so much, Nora," she sobbed.

To get out of the workhouse, Nora had to tear herself away from Sally. A footman accompanied her to the residence of Lady

Alva. The mansion had several levels and a large, expansive garden. Until then, Nora hadn't come across anything like it.

In the foyer, Lady Alva awaited her arrival. She stood tall and beautiful, her silver hair framing her gentle face. It was with a warm greeting that she greeted Nora. "May you find much joy in this new home."

No matter how hard Nora tried, she couldn't fake her own genuine happiness. Despite her appreciation to Lady Alva, she couldn't help but feel sad about leaving Sally behind.

Nora was shown to her tiny, but clean and tidy, chamber by Lady Alva. Lady Alva informed her that she wanted to have her begin working the next day. The time to relax and settle down had come.

Nora had slept little that night, as her thoughts were preoccupied with worry for Sally. Despite Lady Alva's hospitality and the warmth of her bed, she could not shake the feeling that something was amiss.

Nora returned to the workhouse immediately following her half-day off. She tried to maintain a positive attitude so that she could cheer Sally up when she saw her. However, as she entered the workhouse, she could hear Sally's sobs echoing throughout the halls.

Nora dashed to the room where Sally was being held, her heart breaking at the sight of her sister huddled in a corner, her face streaked with tears. Nora approached her and presented the bread and cheese she had brought from Lady Alva's residence.

Sally sniffled and wiped her eyes because her hunger had overcome her pride. She graciously accepted the food and savoured every bite.

Nora could not bear to see her sister in such agony, but she knew there was nothing she could do. The matron was a harsh woman, quick to punish even the smallest transgression. Nora could only hope that in the future, Sally would learn to be more cautious.

Nora attempted to reassure Sally that the situation would improve while they ate. In an effort to cheer her up, she told her about Lady Alva's kindness. Sally remained despondent, clinging to Nora as if she feared letting her go.

Nora stayed as long as she could, but it was eventually time for her to return to Lady Alva's home. Nora had no choice but to depart despite Sally's pleadings. As they said their goodbyes, she assured Sally that she would return as soon as possible.

As soon as Nora was outside, she took a deep breath and attempted to suppress her tears. She knew she had to be brave for Sally's sake, but she was finding it harder and harder to maintain her optimism.

While she made her way back to Lady Alva's home, Nora could not stop thinking about Sally's tear-streaked face. When she first began working there, she was filled with optimism, assuming that her good fortune would extend to her sister. Sally's condition at the workhouse, though, was a vivid reminder of how little control they had over their lives.

Nora attempted to dispel her gloomy thoughts as she approached the huge mansion. Lady Alva's generosity had been a highlight of her life, and she did not wish to take it for granted.

"Welcome back, Nora," Lady Alva replied with a friendly smile. "How is your sister doing?"

Nora's heart sunk upon recalling Sally's predicament. "She's still suffering, Ma'am. The matron is extremely rigorous, and Sally appears to struggle to keep up with the job."

Lady Alva's expression became grave. "Nora, I'm sad to hear that. Is there anything that I can do to assist?"

Nora gave a headshake. "I appreciate your concern, Ma'am, but I don't believe anyone can do anything. I believe Sally needs to learn to keep her head down and work harder."

Lady Alva regarded Nora with worry. "Nora, it is not that simple. No one should have to endure such suffering. I will chat with my husband to determine whether we can offer any assistance."

Nora was moved by Lady Alva's thoughtfulness, but she did not wish to get her hopes up. Sally was essentially confined in the workhouse, with no apparent means of escape.

Nora immersed herself in her work as the days passed, attempting to concentrate on the positive aspects of her life. Lady Alva remained sympathetic to her, providing her modest snacks and encouraging words. Nora began to sense a glimmer of hope that she could possibly establish a life for herself in this location.

But as she reflected on her sister, her optimism waned. Sally's circumstances at the workhouse appeared to be deteriorating. She was being chastised more frequently, and her frail body began to appear malnourished.

On her half-days off, Nora visited her sister as frequently as possible, giving her any extra food she could find. Nonetheless, it was difficult for her to conceal her misery from Sally, who appeared to know that her sister was hurting.

While Nora was working one day, one of the other maids informed her, "Lady Alva wishes to see you."

Nora's pulse pounded faster with each step as she made her way through the stately hallways of Lady Alva's mansion. She wondered why Lady Alva wanted to see her. Was it regarding Sally? Could she finally offer assistance to her sister?

Nora took a deep breath as she approached Lady Alva's study and knocked on the door.

"Enter," Lady Alva's voice said.

As Nora entered the room, she observed the beautiful furnishings and book-lined shelves. Lady Alva was seated at her desk with a stack of papers before her.

"Oh, Nora," murmured Lady Alva with a loving smile. "Thank you for coming."

Nora could not help but have some anxiety. Lady Alva was always polite to her, but she remained a wealthy and influential woman. "Of course, Ma'am. Is there anything you require?"

Lady Alva indicated that she should take a seat in one of the chairs in front of her desk.

"There indeed is. Your sister, Sally, and her circumstances at the workhouse have been on my mind. It is very unacceptable for her to be treated that cruelly."

Nora's pulse raced in response to Lady Alva's comments. Might Lady Alva have found a way to assist Sally after all?

"I've discussed it with my husband," Lady Alva added, "And I've decided to assist Sally in leaving the workhouse and find her a better living situation."

Nora felt tears appear in her eyes. She was shocked. Lady Alva and her husband wanted to assist Sally? It was the realisation of a dream.

Nora's voice choked with emotion as she murmured, "Thank you, Ma'am. Thank you incredibly. I am at a loss for words to express my thanks."

Lady Alva smiled sweetly. "Nora, there's no need to thank me. It is simply the correct action to take. We will contact our contacts in the city to determine if any positions are available for Sally. We will offer her financial assistance until she is able to maintain herself."

Nora smiled softly. It resembled a miracle. Sally could leave the workhouse and begin a fresh life. All of this was due to Lady Alva and her husband.

Nora's voice was trembling as she addressed Lady Alva. "Please, Ma'am. Please let me know if I can be of assistance in any way. I want to do everything I can to reciprocate your generosity."

Lady Alva smiled sweetly. "Nora, you've already accomplished so much. Your diligence and perseverance have not gone unnoticed. But I will consider your offer. Why don't you now take the remainder of the day off? Visit with your sister. And kindly extend our regards to her."

Nora rose to her feet, her heart filled with thankfulness. "Thank you, Ma'am. I will. I cannot express my gratitude enough."

Lady Alva gestured dismissively with her hand. "Nora, no need to thank me. It is what any reasonable individual would do."

Nora departed Lady Alva's study as if she was floating on air. She couldn't wait to tell Sally the wonderful news in person. She would be able to escape the workhouse and begin a new life thanks to Lady Alva's generosity.

Nora returned to the workhouse with a lighter heart than she had felt in weeks.

She went directly to Sally's dorm upon her arrival, but she was not there. Nora asked one of the other girls if she had seen Sally and was informed that Sally had been taken to the infirmary earlier that day.

Nora's heart dropped. What had transpired with Sally? Was she okay? She hurried to the infirmary, her mind racing with anxiety.

She noticed Sally lying on a cot with her eyes closed when she arrived. She was being cared for by a nurse who was monitoring her pulse and taking notes.

Nora approached the nurse and spoke with a trembling voice. "Is she all right? What's wrong with her?"

The nurse looked up with a friendly but strong expression. "She is well, Miss. She just passed out. It has been occurring frequently lately. We believe that poor diet and severe working circumstances are to blame."

Nora was overcome by a surge of wrath. How could they treat individuals in such a manner? How could they disregard their pain?

"May I sit next to her?" Nora inquired, pointing to Sally.

The nurse gave a nod. "Of course. Nonetheless, I must request that you be quiet. We have additional patients who require rest."

Nora nodded and sat down beside Sally's cot. She softly grasped her sister's hand and squeezed it. "Can you hear me, Sally? It's Nora."

Sally opened her eyes. "Nora? Why…"

"I came to see you," Nora stated with a smile. "And I have good news for you. Lady Alva and her husband have made the decision to assist you. They will get you out of the workhouse and into a better situation."

Sally's eyes grew wider. "They are going to assist me?"

Nora nodded. "Indeed they are. They will find you a job and provide you with money until you can sustain yourself."

Sally's eyes swelled with tears. "I find it unbelievable. Finally, after all this time, something positive is occurring."

Nora grinned. "Indeed, it is. All of this is due to Lady Alva and her husband."

Sally's expression became solemn. "How can I ever thank her, Nora? No one has ever been so kind to me."

Nora nodded, certain that her sister was correct. "I know. We are fortunate to have her help or things would continue to be dire for you at the workhouse. Now, let's concentrate on getting you out of here."

Sally nodded, her eyes closing again. "Okay. Many thanks, Nora. Thank you incredibly."

Nora continued to sit with her sister until she fell asleep. Afterwards, she left the infirmary in silence.

When she arrived at Lady Alva's home, she was notified that Lady Alva was absent, but that her husband was in his office and wanted to speak with her.

Nora approached Lord Colby's office with trepidation, but she took a deep breath and knocked on the door.

Chapter 4

Nora waited with her pulse racing outside Lord Colby's study. She had never spoken with him before, so she was uncertain of what to expect. She questioned whether he would be as nice and empathetic as Lady Alva.

The door opened after a minute, and Lord Colby stood there. He was a tall, intimidating man with angular features and a severe demeanour. Nora felt a shudder go down her spine as he regarded her with a cold glare.

"What do you want?" he said in a harsh tone.

Nora took a deep breath, attempting to maintain her composure. "I'm Nora, Sir. Sally's sister. Lady Alva had agreed to assist us, but she has been called away on an emergency. I had hoped, instead, that you could assist us."

Lord Colby's face became gloomier. "I see. And what type of assistance do you need?"

Nora inhaled deeply and gathered her thoughts. "My sister is quite ill. According to the nurses, her frequent fainting is a result of the bad circumstances at the workhouse. Lady Alva promised to get Sally a job and provide her with money to sustain herself until she is fit to work, but she had to depart before she could make the necessary arrangements. I had hoped that you could perform the task instead."

Lord Colby narrowed his eyes. "I see. Why should I assist you?"

Nora had a burst of rage. How could he be so indifferent? "Because you are a wealthy man with the ability to influence the lives of others. Because my sister is ill and needs assistance. Because Lady Alva promised to assist us, and I believe she intended to keep her word."

Lord Colby's cold expression relaxed slightly. "I see. I will have to discuss this with my wife. I am uncertain of her intentions, but I will do all I can."

Nora sensed a glimpse of optimism. "Thank you, Sir. I appreciate it."

With a nod from the Lord, Nora prepared to leave. When she did so, she heard him calling her. "Miss?"

Nora looked around with a lump in her throat. "Yes, Sir?"

Lord Colby regarded her with a focused stare. "I am aware of your worry for your sister's well-being. But you must acknowledge that our capabilities are limited. We are unable to save everyone. Yet occasionally, sacrifices are necessary for the larger good."

Nora experienced a shiver down her spine. What was he trying to say? Was he implying that he wouldn't assist Sally? She was speechless, so she merely nodded and exited the room.

With her thoughts racing, Nora returned to the staff quarters. Her unease at Lord Colby's words made her worry that he wouldn't be of much use to her and Sally. When Lady Alva was absent, Nora felt helpless, despite knowing that she was their greatest chance.

Nora did her best during the following three weeks to fulfil her role as a domestic worker in the Colby family. Yet, the animosity she was beginning to feel was too strong to dismiss. She appreciated Lady Alva's hospitality, but she felt like a prisoner in the mansion.

Nora came up with the brilliant plan to willfully botch her assignments. It was Nora's fondest wish that Lady Alva would get tired of her antics and return her to the workhouse.

Nora knew she was taking a chance, but she saw no other options.

To begin, she failed to thoroughly clean the cutlery, resulting in smudges and blemishes. Nora feigned remorse and promised to do better the next time when Lady Alva reprimanded her. She purposely shattered one of Lady Alva's fine porcelain cups the next day. Angry at Nora, Lady Alva demanded an apology, and she accepted Nora's offer to cover the cost of a new one.

Nora kept making blunders in the hopes that Lady Alva would let her go. However, Lady Alva kept her cool and didn't explode into anger. She encouraged Nora to keep trying and offered to show her the right way to do things. An uncomfortable feeling of remorse arose in Nora. Lady Alva meant well by her offer of assistance, but Nora was actively working against her.

When Lady Alva caught Nora purposely drenching the kitchen floor with water, her anger was evident.

"What are you doing?" she asked in a harsh tone.

A lump began to form in Nora's throat. She was lost for words and unsure of how to explain herself without giving away her genuine motives.

"Pardon me for the inconvenience, Lady Alva. I didn't intend to do that."

Lady Alva gave her a knowing glance. "I know you're disappointed with Sally's life at the workhouse, Nora. Yet, under no circumstances will it be helpful to sabotage your own efforts. We must discuss the issue at hand and work towards a mutually agreeable resolution."

To Nora's humiliation, she realised that Lady Alva was correct. She needed to grow up and learn that her childish behaviour had real repercussions.

"Please accept my apologies, Lady Alva. I intend to improve."

There was a nod of approval from Lady Alva. "Good. And don't be shy about asking for help if you need it. Please let us know how we can assist you."

Nora felt ashamed and left the room. She was completely transparent to Lady Alva. She was angry with herself for believing her scheme would succeed. But she was unable to give up. She needed to convince Lady Alva to return her to the workhouse.

Nora grew increasingly determined to return to the workhouse with her sister Sally as the days passed. She was aware that deliberately botching her tasks was risky, but she saw no other way out of her predicament. Nora had to find a way out of Lady Alva's estate, where she felt like an outsider in a world of luxury and excess.

Nora's plan to commit errors continued, and she hoped that Lady Alva would eventually lose patience with her and return her to the workhouse. However, Lady Alva was not a typical lady. She was kind, patient, and understanding, and rather than reprimand Nora, she attempted to teach her the proper way to conduct herself.

While Nora was dusting the library shelves one afternoon, Lady Alva approached her with a gentle smile. "Dear Nora, I've noticed that you've been having trouble with your work recently. Is everything okay?"

Nora was taken aback by Lady Alva's gracious words. She had anticipated a stern reprimand rather than genuine concern. "I...I'm fine, Lady Alva, thank you for asking," she replied, with a twinge of remorse for lying to the kind-hearted woman.

Lady Alva placed a reassuring hand on Nora's shoulder. "I'm glad to hear that. However, if you need assistance with anything, please don't hesitate to ask. We're all here to support you."

Nora was unable to believe it. Lady Alva offered her assistance, despite the fact that she knew Nora was intentionally making mistakes. Nora's heart swelled with both appreciation and regret.

She desired to divulge all of her secrets and beg for forgiveness from Lady Alva, but she was unable to do so. She feared the consequences and what Lady Alva would think of her.

"I'll keep that in mind, Lady Alva." Nora attempted to sound as appreciative as possible.

Lady Alva smiled warmly and walked away, leaving Nora conflicted and embarrassed. She knew she was doing something wrong, but she was unable to stop. She needed to find a way to return to Sally so that she and her sister could begin a new life together.

Nora continued to sneak into the workhouse on her half-day off to visit Sally over the course of the weeks. Sally was always pleased to see her sister, but Nora could tell that Sally was becoming increasingly impatient with their situation. She could see the desire for a better life beyond the confines of the workhouse in Sally's eyes.

However, Nora was unable to share her plan with Sally. She didn't want to get her hopes up in case the plan failed. She did not wish to disappoint her sister.

***

Nora's plan to make mistakes and be sent back to the workhouse continued as the days turned into weeks. She purposefully made careless mistakes, spilling tea on the fine carpets and breaking valuable things. Lady Alva, on the other hand, remained patient and kind, always offering to help and teach her the proper way to do things.

Nora became increasingly irritated. Lady Alva should have given up on her by now and sent her back to the workhouse, but instead, the woman seemed more determined than ever to assist her. Nora wasn't sure how much longer she could keep up the act.

Nora accidentally spilled hot liquid all over Lord Colby's lap while serving tea to Lady Alva and her husband. He jumped up, cursing and yelling, and Lady Alva rushed to his aid.

Nora was in a terrible situation. She didn't mean to hurt anyone, but her plan had gone too far. She'd made a mistake that was difficult to forgive.

"What is the meaning of this, girl?" Lord Colby screamed, his face flushed with rage.

"I apologise, sir. It was a mistake, "Nora stammered, the weight of her guilt pressing down on her.

"This is intolerable!" Lady Alva stated sternly as she assisted her husband to his feet, "I've tried to be patient with you, Nora, but this is the final straw. You've made too many mistakes, and we can't tolerate it any longer. I'm afraid we'll have to let you go."

Nora's heart broke. She had hoped for this outcome, however, now that it had occurred, she felt regret and sadness. She didn't want to leave Lady Alva's home, but she had to return to the workhouse to see her sister.

"Lady Alva, I apologise for causing you so much trouble," Nora said while fighting back tears.

"I'm sorry it had to end this way, Nora. You could have had a promising future here, but you chose to waste it all," Lady Alva said, her face a mix of disappointment and sympathy.

Nora could only nod, unable to speak. She was well aware that she had committed a grave mistake, but she had no choice. She had to return to the workhouse to see Sally.

Nora couldn't resist thinking of Sally as she packed her meagre possessions. She hoped her sister would be delighted to see her, but she knew life in the workhouse would be difficult. She had firsthand knowledge of the arduous work and scant food that awaited her.

Despite the difficulties, Nora was determined to improve her, and Sally's, lives. She'd find a way out of the workhouse no matter what. And she knew she could overcome anything with Sally by her side.

Chapter 5

Nora felt a twinge of sadness as she said her goodbyes to Lady Alva and Lord Colby. She knew she'd miss the opulent surroundings and warm-hearted people she'd grown to know, but she also knew her heart belonged with Sally in the workhouse. She had to make it work for the sake of both of them.

"I apologise, Lady Alva. I'll never forget your generosity, "Nora's voice trembled with emotion.

"Nora, I hope you find what you're looking for. And I hope you remember what you've learned here," Lady Alva said and smiled sadly at her.

With a nod, Nora left the house, prepared to take on whatever awaited her. She had made a mistake; however, she was determined to make it right.

Nora headed towards the workhouse on the long dirt road. Her steps were heavy, her heart weighed down by the thought of leaving Lady Alva's home. She couldn't help but feel a pang of regret for her mistakes, but she knew she needed to return to the workhouse to be with Sally.

The sky was a warm orange colour as the sun set behind her. The leaves rustled under her feet, and the air was cool as she walked. Nora's heart started to beat faster as she got closer to the workhouse.

The smell of stale bread and wet blankets greeted Nora as she entered the workhouse. She approached the matron's office, her heart racing. The matron looked up at her with a cold, unwelcoming expression as she walked in.

"Well, well, well, look who's coming back in a crawl," the matron said with disdain.

"I sincerely apologise." Nora forced herself to take a deep breath and gather her composure. "I apologise for my mistakes and am committed to making things better."

"Don't worry; you'll have plenty of opportunities to work hard. But first, I have some bad news to share with you," the matron said.

"What news?" Nora's heartbeat quickened.

The matron looked at her with a pitying expression on her face. "Your sister, Sally, has been sent away."

"Sent away? Where?" Nora inquired, her voice trembling.

"To work as a maid in the home of a wealthy merchant, Mr Oscar Bradley," the matron said venomously, "She's been gone for a week."

Nora's thoughts raced. She couldn't believe Sally had been taken away from her yet again. She had hoped to be reunited with her sister so they could work together to make a better life for themselves.

"Why didn't anyone inform me?" Nora inquired with anger.

"I assumed you were aware." The matron shook her head then explained, "It is not my responsibility to keep you updated on your sister's whereabouts."

Nora felt a surge of rage and frustration well up inside her. She knew the workhouse did not care about its residents' well-being, but she had hoped that the matron would have had some decency.

"I need to see her," Nora stated emphatically.

"You cannot simply walk into Mr Bradley's house and demand to see your sister." The matron gave her a sneer. "You, like everyone else, will have to wait until visiting day."

Nora felt a sense of hopelessness wash over her. She knew that visiting day was still two weeks away, and she couldn't bear the thought of having to wait that long to see Sally.

"Is there anything you can do, please?" Nora begged.

"No. Now, it's time to get to work. We have a lot of work to do today," the matron said and shrugged her shoulders.

With her head racing, Nora rushed out of the office. Without Sally, she was not sure how she would make it. She had hoped that they would be able to work together to escape the workhouse and build a better life for themselves, but now she was alone.

Nora was overcome with emotion as she made her way to the laundry room. She needed to hear Sally's laughter and feel her loving embrace again.

Nora had been deeply affected by the news that Sally had left, and she was unable to escape the loneliness that had crept in.

Every day was difficult. She went to work in the laundry room after waking up early and eating a little meal. The other girls weren't nice, and the job was difficult. As she entered the room, they muttered to themselves while glaring at her. During her last stay at the workhouse, Nora had made enemies, but she couldn't recall what she had done to make them hate her.

She worked hard, trying to keep her mind occupied with the monotonous task of washing clothes. But her thoughts kept returning to Sally. She was curious about what her sister was doing and whether or not she was safe and happy. Sally was tough, but Nora couldn't help but worry about her.

Nora was assigned to clean the floors on the third day. She was given a bucket of soapy water and a rag and told to scrub each room until they were spotless. It was a difficult task, but Nora was determined to complete it successfully. She scuffed the floors until her hands were red and sore from working so hard.

As Nora was cleaning up in the final room, she heard a noise in the corridor. She peered out the door and observed a group of girls congregating around something.

Curiosity overcame her, and she strolled over to see what was going on.

A girl of no more than ten years old stood in the middle of the group. She was crying, her cheeks red and swollen from crying. Nora recognised her as the girl who had recently arrived at the workhouse. She had overheard the other girls say that she was too weak for the tasks and would soon be sent away because of that.

"What is happening?" Nora asked as she pushed through the crowd.

The other girls mocked her, but she ignored them. She approached the child and crouched down next to her.

"What is wrong?" Nora inquired softly.

With tears rolling down her face, the young girl turned to face her. "I can't do it. I can no longer work. I'm so exhausted, and my hands hurt," she said, her voice trembling.

Nora felt a flash of sympathy for the beautiful girl. She understood how it felt to be overwhelmed and exhausted. She rested her hand on the young girl's shoulder.

"It's all right," Nora said softly, "Let's go see the matron. Perhaps she can offer you a break."

The other girls rolled their eyes and scoffed, but Nora ignored them. She assisted the small girl in getting up and took her to the matron's office.

The matron was not delighted to see them when they arrived. She stared at Nora before turning her gaze to the small child.

"What's the problem?" the matron said, her voice chilly.

Fear filled the small girl's eyes as she stared up at the matron. "I'm unable to work any longer. My hands hurt, and I'm exhausted."

The matron laughed. "You'll have to disregard that. Laziness is not tolerated here."

Nora's anger began to increase. This was the type of treatment that had prompted her to leave the workhouse in the first place. She spoke out, her voice forceful.

"She's just a kid," Nora explained, "She's exhausted and in pain. Can't you please give her a break?"

As Nora listened to the matron's harsh words, she felt her blood boil. She couldn't believe somebody could be so cruel to a sick child. She knew she had to help the young girl, but she also knew she couldn't do it alone.

"I'll take care of her," Nora stated emphatically, "I'll make sure she gets some rest and gets back to work as soon as she can."

The matron raised an eyebrow, evidently taken aback by Nora's offer. "Very well," she said at the end, "But if she can't keep up, she'll be sent away like the others."

Nora nodded, knowing that was the best she could hope for. She approached the child and took her hand.

"Come on," Nora invited, "Let me take you to get some rest."

As she gazed up at Nora, the small girl nodded, her tears drying up. She accompanied her out of the matron's office and down the corridor to the dormitory. Nora assisted her onto a bed and wrapped a blanket around her.

"Thanks," the little girl sniffled.

"You are most welcome; what is your name?"

Before responding, the young girl paused for a bit. "Sophie," she quietly said.

"My name is Nora. I'll check on you later, okay?"

Sophie nodded, already falling asleep. Nora stood there for a minute, observing her serene breathing. She couldn't help but worry if Sally was sleeping as well as Sophie.

Nora hurried back to the laundry room, unable to shake the gloom that had descended over her. She missed Sally more than anything.

The rest of the day flew by in a flash. Nora worked tirelessly, trying to keep her mind occupied with the monotony of her tasks. Her thoughts kept returning to Sally and Sophie.

Nora was folding a stack of sheets when she heard talking and laughter outside. When she looked out the window, she noticed a man and a woman walking towards the workhouse. They were dressed formally and appeared out of place in the run-down neighbourhood.

Nora felt an uncomfortable feeling wash over her. She was aware that visitors were unusual at the workhouse, and she couldn't help but wonder what they were doing there.

She walked outside after finishing folding the sheets. She noticed the woman was carrying a small bag as she approached them. It appeared to be full of clothes.

"Excuse me," Nora said hesitantly, "Can I assist you?"

The woman smiled warmly as she looked at her. "Yes, indeed. We are looking for a girl. Sophie is her name. We've been told she is here."

Nora felt a knot in her stomach. She was well aware of who they were looking for.

"I'm sorry," Nora apologised softly, "Sophie isn't feeling well. She's sleeping in the dorm."

"Oh, no. Is she okay?" The woman's smile began to fade.

Nora gave a nod. "She simply needs to rest. Is there anything else I can do to assist you?"

The woman gave her a brief glance before nodding. "Actually, yes. We've come to pick her up. She's been hired as a maid in the home of Mr Oscar Bradley, a wealthy merchant."

Nora's heart sank when she heard the woman mention Oscar Bradley's name. It was the same name that haunted Nora every night. Her mind was racing as she listened to the woman's request.

"I'm sorry," Nora said, her voice trembling with desperation, "But Sophie is too young and weak to work as a maid. She's barely strong enough to do the laundry here."

The woman gave her a worried look. "I have no choice; we were told to pick her up and take her to Mr Bradley's home."

Nora paused for only a moment. "Actually, the workhouse has a policy that any girl who leaves must be replaced by someone else. Maybe I could take Sophie's place and work as a maid in her place?"

"And how do we know you're qualified for the job?" The woman regarded Nora with skepticism.

"I have domestic work experience, and I can provide you with a letter of reference from the workhouse matron to prove it," Nora said and breathed deeply, hoping that her plan would work.

The woman gave her a brief glance before nodding. "Very well. But first, we will need to see that letter."

"Yes, Ma'am. I will have the matron write it and will take it to Mr Bradley's within 2 days." Nora couldn't look at the woman, fearing she would see the deceit in her eyes.

"Very well. But if we do not see that letter in 2 days, we will have to come back for Sophie."

Nora's heart raced as she watched the man and woman walk away. She knew that she had to act quickly if she wanted to see Sally again. She didn't want to think about what would happen to Sally if she didn't get to work for Oscar Bradley.

Nora ran to the laundry room, her mind buzzing with a plan. She would forge a letter of reference from the workhouse matron, then go to Mr Bradley's townhouse and apply for a position as a maid.

The next day, Nora skipped her lunch, choosing to focus on the letter. She sat down at one of the worktables and began to write the letter of reference. It was not an easy task, but Nora had no other choice. She needed to convince the Bradley family that she was a qualified domestic worker who could be trusted with their home and their children, if they had any.

After several attempts, Nora finally finished the letter. She read it over, making sure it was convincing and believable. Satisfied, she folded the paper and tucked it into her pocket before leaving the workhouse.

Chapter 6

Nora took a deep breath as she looked at the house where Sally now worked. Her hand shook gently as she took in her surroundings. While not as elegant as Lady Alva's home, Mr Bradley's home left Nora in awe. At least Sally had a nice place to live. Nora only hoped that the work wasn't too hard for her and that Sally was treated kindly.

Closing her eyes and momentarily being sorry for forging the letter of reference, Nora gripped the small bag in her hand, the only possessions she owned, and knocked on the door. After confirming who she was, Nora was led inside and straight to Mrs Emsworth, the housekeeper. Nora recognised her from being at the workhouse earlier. As she looked

Nora up and down, Nora nervously handed Mrs Emsworth the letter of reference.

"Hmm," was all Mrs Emsworth said as she read the letter a second time.

Nora smiled nervously and looked around. She was eager to see Sally but she had to keep her composure.

"You sound like a good fit, Nora," Mrs Emsworth said, glancing coldly at her. "We do need a new maid since Elsa ran off with that no good footman next door. I never did trust him, and I suspected there was something going on between those two but I could never prove it."

"I see, uh, thank you, Mrs Emsworth." Nora said a silent prayer. She was in! She had the job. Most importantly, she would see her sister again.

"Think nothing of it," Mrs Emsworth spoke in her cool, icy voice. "You are highly recommended by the matron, and I trust her opinion as I know Mr Bradley would as well. Now, I expect you to work hard, mind your manners, and not be going off with a footman after hours. If I get word of that, you will be dismissed immediately. Do you understand?"

"Yes, Ma'am," Nora replied, "I won't be a burden to you. I assure you."

"Good. Now can you start today?"

Nora nodded.

"I will show you to your room. There are 3 other girls you will be sharing a room with.

Work hard, girl, and you won't have any problems here. Understood?"

"Of course, Ma'am. Thank you for this."

Mrs Emsworth nodded and motioned for Nora to follow her up the stairs. Off to the right, Nora was led into a small room with 4 cots. While it wasn't as nice as the room she'd had at Lady Alva's, it was clean and warm, and much better than the workhouse.

"Now unpack your things and meet me downstairs. I'll get Sally to leave your uniform on your bed. You may take 30 minutes to unpack and dress, then you'll need to get to work."

"Yes, Ma'am." Nora smiled at Mrs Emsworth and was shocked to get a smile in return. With a nod of her head, Mrs Emsworth turned to leave, almost banging into someone as she exited the room.

"My apologies, Ma'am, I didn't see you."

Nora's heart skipped a beat as she recognised that voice. Her sister!

"Sally, we've hired a new maid. Get a uniform for her and bring it to her. Bring her downstairs in 30 minutes so she can start work. I expect you to help her until she gets used to things around here."

"Of course, Ma'am."

Mrs Emsworth walked out of view and Nora had a brief glimpse of Sally as she turned to the left and walked away.

It felt like hours before Sally appeared with a uniform in her hands. Not even looking at Nora, Sally walked past her and placed the uniform on the bed with Nora's bag.

"Thank you, Sally," Nora said softly.

"Of course. And you..." Sally stopped speaking when she saw that it was Nora standing in front of her. "Nora?! Nora! What are you doing here?"

"Sally! I... I've been hired on as a maid here. Oh, Sally, look at you! You look good. Are they treating you well here? Are you able to do the work? It's not too hard on you is it?"

Sally couldn't answer Nora as tears rolled down her cheeks. "Oh, Nora, I thought I'd never see you again. I didn't want to come here because I was afraid you'd never find me. But this was the one good thing that's happened to me, Nora. The other girls are nice and so is Mrs Emsworth, once you get to know her. The work is, well... work, but I can do it. It's so much better than the workhouse, Nora, so much better."

Nora wrapped her arms around Sally. "Oh, Sally, I was so worried about you. I would have done whatever it took to find you, but the matron told me where you were. One of the other girls at the workhouse was supposed to come here but she is sickly and the work here would have been too much for her, so... I decided to come in her place. I packed my bag and left, praying that they would let me work here, and they have. Sally, I promise you, I will never leave you again. We will always stick together; always be together."

Sally wiped her tears. "Always, Nora, it will always be us. We won't allow anyone to separate us again. Now, you better unpack and get dressed in your uniform. If Mrs Emsworth says be downstairs in 30 minutes, well, you better be downstairs in 30 minutes."

Nora looked at Sally, and they both laughed.

"Really, Nora, Mrs Emsworth will grow on you. She may come off as cold and grouchy but she's really not. But she does expect the work to get done when it should, and she doesn't tolerate mistakes very well. But if you do your best, do your work, and are helpful and punctual, you'll be fine here."

Nora hoped Sally was right. Nora knew she would do whatever it took to stay with Sally. If the work was hard, or if the hours were long, Nora was willing to pay that price to never be separated from her sister again.

***

Nora finished cleaning the parlour, her back letting her know she should have taken a quick break. But Nora feared that Mrs Emsworth would catch her, and the punishment of working an hour longer than anyone else would make her back hurt even more.

A month had passed since Nora had arrived at the Bradley house. While the work was hard, it was much better than the workhouse, and Nora was thankful for that every day. Mrs Emsworth seemed to enjoy handing off more tasks to Nora than she did the other girls. But the lady's iciness seemed to have eased a little bit, and Nora felt herself grow under Mrs Emsworth's tutelage.

Nora and the other maids found Mr Bradley to be harsh and rigid. While he rarely acknowledged the maids, he made it a point to acknowledge if something wasn't to his liking. Nora had encountered Mr Bradley's wrath several times. She had learnt over the past month that Mr Bradley wanted his home to be spotless, and even a speck of dust in his favourite room, the parlour, could set him off.

When Nora witnessed Della, one of the other maids, being chastised by Mr Bradley one day for not cleaning the parlour to his high standards, Nora had stepped in, defending Della and offering to take over the cleaning of that room.

Mr Bradley had looked at her, a sneer on his face, before dismissing Della.

"Very well, but I do not appreciate being made to look a fool in front of the staff, Miss. I sure hope your cleaning skills are good and up to my expectations. If so, I will ignore your most inappropriate outburst to me. This is MY home, and I can certainly decide who works here and who doesn't. Keep that in mind, Miss…"

"Nora, Sir. It's Nora. And I do apologise, Sir. It's just, well, I guess I'm always looking out for everyone and I…I felt sorry for…"

"Just watch that mouth of yours, Miss…Nora. And mind your place. You are nothing but a lowly maid here and I can certainly have you thrown out. Would you prefer the workhouse to being here?"

Nora felt sick. She would never go back to the workhouse. She'd go to Lady Alva and beg for her job back, with Sally by her side, before she'd set foot in the workhouse again. And Nora didn't want Sally to pay the price because of her outburst.

"Yes, Sir. It won't happen again. I…I do like it here. I'm a hard worker and…"

"Get to it, girl. I'll be keeping an eye on you."

Nora wiped a tear away when Mr Bradley walked away. It was in Nora's soul to want to help people. She had seen the terror in Della's eyes when Mr Bradley had reprimanded her, and she had stepped in to remedy the situation before she had a chance to even think about it.

You have to learn to think only about yourself and Sally. Do you want to be put back out on the street with nowhere to go? Do you want to be separated from Sally?

Those thoughts are what kept Nora cleaning the parlour until it was spotless. And Mrs Emsworth still expected Nora to do her other tasks as well. Nora saw the look of disdain on Mrs Emsworth's face and the shaking of her head every time she checked on Nora in the parlour. Nora learnt to avert her eyes and keep cleaning.

The only bright spot of the day was when all of the maids were in their room at night. The girls often whispered about Mr Bradley and Mrs Emsworth, but all were grateful that they had a warm place to stay. Sally flourished with Nora there, and Nora was impressed with how far Sally had come. She was growing up and was a hard worker.

As the days turned into weeks, Nora seemed to have gained the respect of Mrs Emsworth, who told her that she needed to just do her work and not try to save everyone.

"The other girls are happy to have a warm and safe place to work and live, Nora. Yes, the work can be hard, but you have to be grateful for what you have. I know the workhouse was hard, but you're not there anymore. Do you want to go back there? I think not. You're a hard worker, Nora, that's all that I, and Mr Bradley, want. But things can change at any time, so take my advice –

continue to do a good job and you will be treated well here."

"Yes, Ma'am. It's just in my nature to want to help everyone; to take the burden off of others if I see someone being treated harshly. That's hard to overcome."

"I understand, Nora. But we can't help others all the time, can we? Sometimes, we just have to take care of ourselves. Della would have learnt to do a better job if you had just let things be. Now, you've had to take on additional work besides the normal tasks that are assigned to you. I've seen your pain, Nora, both physical and mental. Do your work, be respectful to Mr Bradley, and you will continue to have a safe place to rest your head at night. And you are with your sister. That should be more than enough, Nora."

Nora knew Mrs Emsworth was right. It was time for her to think of herself, and Sally, instead of worrying about the other two maids who could certainly take care of themselves. Nora knew if she had to take on more work it would likely physically break her, and she would be sent away without a second thought, living on the streets where anything could happen to her.

As she did every day since starting work at Mr Bradley's Nora wished that she had handled things differently with Lady Alva. At the time, making intentional mistakes had seemed the best idea for getting back to the workhouse with Sally. But it had been stupid. Nora had broken the trust of someone who had treated her very well. Perhaps, had she been a better worker towards the end, Lady Alva and her husband may have hired Sally as well. Nora knew their lives would have been much better there, but that was in the past.

Nora had thought she was doing the right thing at the time, but she now knew how stupid she had been. Along with opening her mouth when she shouldn't, Nora now knew she needed to be respectful, work hard, and not speak up unless she absolutely needed to. She was with Sally, and that was why she had left Lady Alva's home in the first place, although Nora wished she had the chance to do it over again and make things right with the Colby's.

***

"I can't believe I've been here three months, Sally," Nora said as the girls got dressed in their uniforms.

"These have been the best three months ever, Nora. I don't know what I would have done if you hadn't come here. The other girls are nice but I missed you terribly. The work is hard but I've gotten used to it. Mrs Emsworth even complimented me the other day on how clean the dishes were. Can you believe it? She's harsh at times but I've seen a softer side to her lately, Nora. And she's much better than that horrid matron."

"Yes, she is. I think even Mr Bradley has softened a bit. Not a lot, but he's not glaring at me anymore and I've not had a complaint that the parlour isn't clean enough. My back sure knows the hard work I do in there, plus the other work that Mrs Emsworth has me do. But the most important part is that we're together with a roof over our heads."

"Oh, Mr Bradley can be horrid, can't he? I'm thankful that I don't see him too much. If I see him coming, I avert my eyes and try to head in the opposite direction. It seems to work as I rarely see him and have never had a run in with him."

"You surely don't want to see his wrath, Sally. It isn't pleasant. But I've come to know that he wants a clean and tidy home. If you work hard, do as you're told, he'll leave you alone. Although it's been hard, I've learnt to count to twenty before I speak up."

Sally giggled. "I know that's hard for you because you always want to take care of everyone. It makes you sad to see someone hurting or scared. You just want to take their pain away. But looked what happened with Mr Bradley when you spoke up for Della,

Nora. He was livid. And now you have much more work to do than we all do. I see you clutching your back every day and wish I could take some of that work from you. Maybe we could talk to Mrs Emsworth and I can help you clean the parlour? I don't mind…"

"No, absolutely not, Sally. It's my fault I have so much work to do. I shouldn't have spoken up. But I did. And as it was me who got myself into this predicament, I'll continue to pay the price. Yes, I work longer than you and the other girls, but I made a promise to you that I would never leave you again, and I will do what I have to to keep that promise. I'll be fine, Sally."

"That makes me sad, Nora, to see you being overworked. But I will not say anything. Just promise me you will let me and the other girls handle our own affairs. I'm not a little girl anymore, Nora, I can take care of myself. Well, not as good as you take care of me, but I have to learn to stand up for myself, Nora. Please, just don't do anything that could have us thrown out on the streets. I don't think I would survive that, Nora. But I would rather die on the streets than go back to that horrid workhouse. And I mean that."

Nora gave her sister a hug. "Don't talk like that, Sally. Nothing like that will happen. I will do the work assigned to me and do it well. I will not speak to Mr Bradley unless spoken to, and I will not try to save everyone else. I know I need to look after us, and I know my actions here reflect on both of us. You have my word, Sally, that I will be on my best behaviour."

"That will be hard for you, Nora," Della chimed in laughing. "I do so appreciate you sticking up for us, but Sally is right. You need to just take care of yourself, Nora. Everything else will fall into place. You'll see."

"I sure hope so, Della. Well, let's get downstairs before Mrs Emsworth comes up to see what's taking us so long. If we're even a minute late we won't get our break in a few hours…"

***

"Happy birthday, Sally!" Nora, Della, and Lucy, the other maid, stood around Sally, beaming as they held out a small gift wrapped in newspaper.

Sally eagerly took it, removing the paper to see a beautiful pink scarf. "Oh I love it, thank you! You know pink is my favourite colour." She put it on, running her fingers lovingly over the carefully knitted scarf.

"We knew you would." Della beamed. "We all took a turn in knitting it, although Lucy did most of it as she's the best knitter."

"How old are you, Sally?" Lucy asked.

"Twelve! Thank you all. I feel very blessed to have you as friends, and Nora as my sister. I'm so happy that we're all together here. That is the best present I could ever ask for."

"And Nora, your birthday is in a few weeks, right? How old will you be?"

"Fourteen. I can't believe how fast time has gone by. My heart still misses Mother and Father but I'm thankful that Sally and I are together. I know that's what they would have wanted."

Nora held back the tears. She didn't want to cry in front of the other girls. Her parents were gone, and there was nothing she could do to bring them back. She'd honour their memory by keeping Sally safe, and making sure they stayed together.

"They would be proud of both of you," Della said. "Lucy and I never had siblings but we're all sisters now. We'll always be here for each other, Nora. Never forget that."

"Come downstairs, girls, I have a surprise for you."

The girls jumped at the unexpected sound of Mrs Emsworth's voice. When she walked away, they all looked at each other. "I hope it's a good surprise," Sally said. "It is my birthday, after all, and I should be able to have a happy one."

As the girls walked downstairs, the smell of baking filled the air. As they walked into the kitchen, a beaming Mrs Emsworth pointed to a small cake on the table. "Happy birthday, Sally."

Nora was shocked, although Sally didn't appear to be. Mrs Emsworth was closer to Sally than the other girls, but her iciness towards Nora had almost disappeared. Nora knew as long as she worked hard, and kept her mouth shut, that she and Mrs Emsworth would get along fine.

Chapter 7

Nora's birthday had been low key, although the girls had knitted her a pair of gloves in her favourite colour, blue. Nora had never been treated so kindly as Della and Lucy treated her. The girls were close and vowed to always support each other. Della had even started to help a little with the parlour cleaning, with Mrs Emsworth's approval. That allowed Nora to only work 30 minutes longer than the other girls, instead of an hour longer. Nora was grateful to Mrs Emsworth and Della for helping her, for the toll of working longer than the other girls had hit Nora hard. With the help from Della, Nora's back started to hurt less, and Nora felt a true happiness she hadn't felt in years.

***

As the holidays approached, Nora and the other girls were instructed by Mrs Emsworth on how to properly clean and prepare for the holidays. With longer work days needed, Nora and Sally learnt to adapt. While the work was harder than they had anticipated, they knew it would only be a few weeks, and their work load would lighten again.

As Nora was dusting the study one day, she felt someone walk into the room. Startled, and expecting an irate Mr Bradley, Nora continued to dust, pretending not to have noticed another presence in the room.

"Excuse me, uh, Miss, do you think you could help me with my bedsheets? I'm afraid I've got them all in a jumble here."

It wasn't Mr Bradley. The voice sounded younger. It was someone Nora had never met before. Was he a new worker?

Taking a breath and then letting it out, Nora turned around. Standing before her was the most handsome boy she had ever seen. Her eyes widened and her heartbeat quickened. For once, Nora was speechless.

"Are you okay? You look quite frightened," he said.

Nora continued to stare. Words formed, but she couldn't get them out. What was happening to her?

"Hello? Are you all right? I didn't mean to startle you."

Nora found her voice. "I…I'm fine."

"Oh, I'm Jack. Jack Bradley. Mr Bradley's son."

"I see." Nora's face reddened and she looked at the floor. She knew it was a bad idea to have these strange feelings for Mr Bradley's son. Nothing good could ever come of it. But she couldn't control the butterflies in her stomach or the rapid beating of her heart.

"And... you are?"

"The maid. Well, one of the maids. That's all." Nora's voice was barely a whisper. She couldn't even look at him. Jack, that was his name. She couldn't even look at Jack.

"What is your name," he pressed, and Nora looked up into the bluest eyes she had ever seen. Blue, her favourite colour. Why did he have to have blue eyes?

"Nora," she whispered softly.

"It's nice to meet you, Nora."

Nora dared to look at Jack again, and their eyes locked. There was something about Jack, something that Nora had never felt before. Nora looked away first, shocked at how bold she had been to stare at Jack like that.

Stop it, Nora. Looking at the master's son like that can get you into trouble. Just be polite and get back to work.

The words were out before Nora could stop them. She couldn't help herself. She was intrigued. "Why haven't I seen you here before?"

Jack's eyes widened in surprise, and he was silent for several minutes before he answered.

Flustered, Nora wished she hadn't spoken up. But it was too late now; the words were out. She silently prayed that Jack wouldn't go to his father and tell him how disrespectful and rude Nora had been. Nora was well aware that the staff shouldn't speak to the home owners unless spoken to first. She prayed her blunder wouldn't cost her a job. Sally would be livid.

"I don't actually live here. Well, at least not very much. My father sent me away to school when I was younger, then he insisted I go to University, which I've just started. I'm only home on holiday break."

"Oh." Nora didn't know what else to say.

"Even on summer break," Jack continued, "My father likes me to stay at University. My father has a business associate in that town, and I'm expected to learn the merchant trade. So I learn over the summer. Which is fine; there's never been much of a reason for me to want to come home in the summer. Holiday break is quite enough; I actually look forward to going back to my studies after break is over."

Nora thought she noted a sad sarcasm in his voice but she dismissed it. She had only just met Jack Bradley, and she didn't want to assume that there was a rift between father and son.

"How long will you be at University?"

"Four long years. My apologies, Nora, I shouldn't have shared so much and bored you. My unhappiness with my life at University and with my father at the moment needn't have been shared."

"I understand, Mr…"

"Please, call me Jack. Mr Bradley is my father," Jack smiled at her.

"Very well, Jack. My pleasure to meet you; no matter how short your stay is here over your holiday break."

Nora felt herself relax as she shared casual chatter with Jack over getting his room in order. His bedsheets were on the bed in no time, and Nora found herself not wanting to leave his room. She hadn't felt this happy since she had been reunited with Sally here.

But this was a foreign happiness, something that Nora had never experienced with a boy before.

Over the next two weeks, Nora and Jack shared secret conversations out of the view of the other staff. Nora learnt that Jack's mother had passed five years earlier, and his father had turned from a loving father into someone that Jack didn't recognise anymore. Jack confided to Nora that he didn't know if the relationship with his father could ever be repaired.

Nora learnt that Jack was two years older than her. At sixteen, he had just started his studies at the University, and she knew he looked forward to being done with his studies, although that was a long four years away. Once he graduated from University, he would get started in his father's business. Jack confided that he wasn't interested in working with his father, but as the Bradley's only child, he was expected to help his father and, eventually, take over the business entirely.

Nora looked forward to seeing Jack each day. She found herself humming as she worked, and her work was much more enjoyable when Jack was around. Jack was always respectful of her and never looked down on her. But Nora knew that there would never be anything but friendship between them. Jack Bradley would never see the lowly household maid as anything more than a friend, no matter how Nora dreamt of a happy future for them.

But such thoughts made her sad, and Nora didn't want to be sad. Her life was going as expected. She and Sally had a roof over their heads and a small wage coming in. They were both thankful for that. Jack had been a bright spot in Nora's life; an unexpected twist of fate that had brightened her life in ways that she could have only imagined.

While Nora thought her meetings with Jack had been well hidden, she was shocked when Sally asked her if she liked Jack – as more than a friend. The girls were alone in the kitchen, and Nora's shocked expression made Sally giggle.

"Oh, Nora, stop! It's written all over your face how you feel about him. I've watched you two in secret, and I've never seen your cheeks have such a rosy glow before. Do you think he likes you too? What do you think Mr Bradley will do if he finds out?"

"Sally, what do you mean you have been watching us in secret? Does anyone else know? Della? Lucy? Or Mrs Emsworth?"

"No! Nora, no, I've never heard anyone else mention it. I just happened to see you with him when I was walking past the study, and I've never seen you look so happy. It made me happy to see you smiling again. It's been a long time, Nora. You're always so serious and protective of me; you just never seemed happy, happy like you were with mother and father. It…I just feel so thankful to Jack for making you feel that way."

"Sally, oh he's so wonderful! I do like him, but we're just friends. Someone like him would never be interested in a girl like me in any other way. I'm just a poor maid, cleaning the house and being paid a wage by his father. Sally, please promise me that you won't say anything to anyone else. If Mr Bradley found out, I'd be out on the streets. And the same with Mrs Emsworth. She'd go to Mr Bradley and I'd be gone. Promise me, Sally."

"Nora, I won't say anything. I promise. I was just so happy to see you smile again, that's all. But from what I saw, Nora, I'd say Jack feels the same way about you as you feel about him – whatever you say it is – friendship or perhaps more."

Nora breathed a sigh of relief. She knew her sister would not tell anyone about her secret meetings with Jack. And she felt much better knowing Mrs Emsworth, Lucy and Della knew nothing about her meetings with

Jack. While Nora knew she felt more than friendship for Jack, she also didn't want to admit that to Sally. For to admit it to Sally would only make her look foolish later when Jack returned to University and never thought about her again. As far as she knew, Jack could already be courting someone. That was one topic they never discussed. And Nora was glad. She'd be heartbroken if she knew Jack had fallen for someone; someone other than her.

***

Nora's and Jack's secret meetings became the highlight of Nora's day. Some days, they'd be able to talk for 10 minutes; other days, they'd give each other a quick smile and wave as they walked past each other when the other girls were nearby.

Although Nora tortured herself with her growing feelings for Jack, she let the tears fall only at night when she was in bed and the other girls were sleeping. She knew he would soon be back at University, and she worried that she would never see him again. He'd confided in her that this was the last holiday he wanted to spend at home as tensions between him and his father were reaching a boiling point.

Nora prayed that Jack would change his mind and come home next year. Of course, she reasoned, she might not even be here next year, but she hoped for the best. As long as she continued to do a good job and work hard, there was little reason to expect that Mr Bradley would let her go. Nora fell asleep with thoughts of Jack disappearing forever, and awoke with fear and dread in her heart.

***

Christmas came faster than Nora had ever thought possible. When Jack insisted that Nora, Sally, Della, Lucy and Mrs Emsworth should share a meal with them, Mr Bradley refused.

"I'm not eating with the help. They're paid a fair wage and have a safe place to live, what else do they want? And what is wrong with you for even suggesting that? I taught you better than that, Jack. Some people have a better life than others, and it's not up to you or me to understand why. I expect you to be polite and courteous to the staff, but I will in no way be sharing a meal with them. You'll learn soon enough when you and I are working together. I expect you to know your worth in life, and that doesn't include befriending the staff."

Nora let out a gasp as she heard Mr Bradley's words. She'd walked past the dining area as she was heading to join the staff for their Christmas meal and had stopped when she'd heard Jack wanting to share the holiday meal with the staff.

Nora shook her head, knowing that what Mr Bradley had said was true. Mr Bradley and Jack were wealthy; they always would be. Neither of them had ever had to work in the horrid workhouse or wondered if they would find a safe place to sleep or food to eat. She and Sally had had a good life when their parents were alive. They were far from wealthy, but they had shelter and food on the table. Now, she and Sally were the lowest of the low, and nothing would ever change Mr Bradley's opinion of them, even though Jack was trying.

Nora prayed that Jack would stay the kind person that he was. Even when he took over his father's business, married and had his own family, Nora prayed that he would remain kind to everyone, no matter how poor or rich they may be.

Nora was glad when the Christmas meal was over, even though the clean-up was taking longer than they'd expected. Mr Bradley had given them the rest of the afternoon off once their chores were completed, and Nora was secretly thankful for time with the girls in their room. As all four girls lay in their beds, they talked about their

Christmas meal and how grateful they were for having a few hours off of work.

Nora half listened to the conversation, her mind playing back Mr Bradley's words of not befriending the lowly servants. But was it too hard to be kind? Did money really matter that much that someone would treat another person without money so horribly?

Lady Alva had never looked down on her staff. She'd treated them as her sons and daughters. Nora's heart ached as she recalled the woman who had taken her in when no one else wanted her. She would always regret leaving there, but Sally would always be her number one priority. But then if she wasn't here, she never would have met Jack. And having a little bit of happiness was like a piece of heaven. Nora knew she would never experience that feeling again in her life with anyone else.

***

"Nora!"

Nora jumped as she was dusting off the books in the library. "Jack! You startled me…"

"I'm sorry, Nora. I saw you in here and saw no one else was around. Did you enjoy your Christmas meal?"

"Yes, thank you. We were all very grateful for the nice meal." She didn't know what else to say. She had to distance herself from Jack as he would be leaving in two days. Her heart was already far too involved with Jack, and she didn't want to endure the heartbreak she knew she would suffer when he walked out the door.

She wished for the hundredth time that things were different. If she were Lady Alva's daughter, she could court Jack. She could fall in love with Jack and look forward to a perfect future with him. Him and their children. She pictured a girl that looked like her and a handsome boy that looked like Jack. How perfect her life could be if she wasn't a servant in his father's house. If she was a somebody from an established and wealthy family, her future would look bright.

"Nora?"

Nora snapped out of her thoughts and looked at Jack. "Yes?"

"You know I'm leaving in two days, don't you?"

"Yes. I hope you have a safe trip back."

Jack's face showed his confusion. "Uh, thanks. What are your future plans, Nora? Do you plan to continue to work for my father?"

"Yes, I suppose so. Sally is here and she's settled, so I wouldn't want to uproot her. I've settled in here as well, and while the work can be taxing at times, it's much better than the workhouse. So, yes, I'm planning to stay here as long as I'm needed, which I hope is a long time."

"I'm sorry, Nora."

"For what?"

"For everything. For what happened to your parents, to you and Sally going to the workhouse, and everything bad that's happened to you. I wish I could take all the sadness you've experienced away from you, but I can't. If I could, I'd take it from you in a heartbeat. The highlight of my day is seeing your beautiful smile. I don't think you see how beautiful, smart and kind you are, Nora. But I do. I'll miss our conversations and your smile when I'm gone."

Nora fought back tears. No one had ever said such kind things to her before. Ever since her parents had left them alone, Nora had been the strong one. As the older sister, she knew it was her job to protect and look after Sally. Life wasn't about just her anymore; she had Sally to care for. And Nora had taken a backseat from caring for, and loving, herself to caring for and loving Sally. For Sally had no one left to care for her, except Nora.

"Nora? I'm sorry if I made you uncomfortable, but I…you're a very special girl, and I never want you to forget that."

"Thank you, Jack. I'll never forget your words and your kindness to me. Ever."

Jack reached for Nora's hand, and his touch felt like a spark of electricity. It frightened her, and she gasped and pulled her hand away. A boy like Jack shouldn't be reaching for her hand. If she was Lady Alva's daughter, it would all make sense. They could talk in public and hold hands whenever they wanted. At least she thought they could. *Could we? I'm not wealthy but do they have to sneak around like Jack and I do? I doubt that they do. But I'll never be wealthy and will never know their way of life.* But sneaking around and having to hide their interactions with each other wasn't how Nora wanted to live. And if Mr Bradley or Mrs Emsworth saw them holding hands, Nora shuddered, not wanting to think about what would happen.

"What's wrong, Nora? I...I didn't mean to frighten you. Here, give me your hand."

She couldn't disobey him. She didn't want to disobey him. She cared about him, and she wanted to do whatever he wanted. Her heart might break, but she didn't care. What mattered, in this moment, was holding her hand out to him, wanting to feel that unfamiliar electric current course through her body.

This time, Nora didn't gasp. She closed her eyes as she felt his warm hand close around her smaller hand. It felt right. The electric shock felt right. Nora knew how she felt about Jack; it didn't matter if he didn't feel the same way back. It was enough to know he cared and thought she was beautiful.

"Keep your eyes closed, Nora," Jack spoke softly.

She trusted him completely, and obeyed him, her feet moving along with Jack's for what seemed like hours but was actually only a few seconds.

"Okay, open them."

Nora opened her eyes and looked around; they were underneath the library door. Confused, she looked up at Jack.

Jack stayed silent as he pointed up to the top of the door frame. Nora looked up to see what looked like part of a plant hanging down the centre of the door frame. She squinted her eyes, trying to get a better look at it, when she felt Jack's hand on her chin, gently pulling her face down. As she looked at him, he leaned in closer, so close that Nora involuntarily took a step back.

Jack gently took her hand and pulled her close to him, and Nora understood. His warm lips brushed hers, very gently at first, and then he kissed her again. Nora's heart raced as she kissed him back. She had never kissed a boy before but with Jack, it felt right. The kiss lasted merely seconds, but to Nora's soul, it went on for eternity. While her head was telling her what a stupid girl she was for falling for Mr Bradley's son, her heart was begging for one more touch, one more kiss from him before he went away and left her heart shattered in a million pieces.

If Nora had any doubt of how she felt about Jack before, that doubt was clarified in their kiss. She had heard about love, and had read books about love, but she didn't believe love could be real. But she knew it now. Even at fourteen, she knew that what she felt for Jack was love, and it was heart breaking to know that he could never feel the same way about her. His father would disown him and society would scorn him.

"Nora?"

She looked up at him with a heavy heart. She didn't want to be foolish and have him see the love she had for him in her eyes. He'd mock her and tell her that it was just a game. That he was wealthy, she was poor, and whatever dalliance they had going on, well it had to stop now. She didn't want to hear that; couldn't bear to hear that.

"Nora?" he said again, and Nora had to look at him. If he saw her feelings for him, she didn't care.

"Yes?" She didn't know what else to say.

"I…you…"

Here it comes. He's going to say that our kiss was a mistake. That he can't have anything to do anymore with a girl like me.

"So, what is that, Jack?" Nora pointed to the plant hanging from the door frame.

"Mistletoe. Do you know what that is?"

Nora laughed. "Oh, I do! My mother and father used to tell Sally and me stories about their first kiss being under mistletoe at Christmas. They said once they shared that kiss, they knew they were meant to be together forever. They said it sealed their fate. They were so happy, Jack, I've never seen two people more in love."

"My mother and father used to be like that. I miss the old days, Nora, when we had happy, loving families. It doesn't seem fair how life can quickly change, does it?"

Nora shook her head, at a loss for words. She didn't want things to change between her and Jack. She wanted this moment to last forever. She wanted another kiss; she wanted him to move back home and care about her forever.

"So, yes, I know what mistletoe is," Nora said softly, her cheeks reddening as she remembered Jack's warm lips on hers. It was a feeling she knew she would always remember.

"Nora, I… I wanted to…"

"Jack! Where are you?" Mr Bradley's voice sounded from down the hallway.

Jack stepped back from Nora, and Nora ran back to the bookshelf, praying that Mr Bradley didn't witness their kiss. Nora suspected if he had, he'd sound a bit more irate than he did.

Nora watched out of the corner of her eye as Mr Bradley entered the library.

"There you are. Come with me, son. We have to arrange your transportation back to

University, and I need some help with a few things before you go."

"Yes, sir. I just walked in here to find a book to take back to University with me, but I'll come back later."

Nora let out a long breath once father and son had left the library. Close. It was too close this time. They had almost gotten caught. She had been so close to being found out and thrown out on the street. Sally would be livid with her. She'd promised to always be with her; she had to let her feelings for Jack go. Her life was here now; Jack would move on and find someone. Maybe she would too, although her heart told her that she'd never feel the same for someone else.

Chapter 8

Nora hadn't been able to see Jack alone before he left. She and the other staff stood in the entryway to bid him goodbye. Nora blinked back the tears. She felt her heart breaking in a million pieces; she felt the happiness leave her soul, and she wondered if she would ever smile again. It hurt, saying goodbye to Jack hurt. She wanted to hug him. To kiss him again. To be close to him. But it wasn't proper for her to do that. So she stood with the others, stone-faced with a breaking heart, wishing him safe travels.

Jack caught her eye a bit longer than he should have, and Nora felt that feeling of deep emotion well up in her. *I love you,* she said silently, hoping he could read her heart and see all the emotions she had for him in her eyes.

Nora looked at the ground, not wanting others to notice the lingering gaze between them. She was the maid; he was the master's son. That was how it was always going to be. Her heart dropped when she saw him enter the carriage. She couldn't bear to see the carriage drive away, carrying Jack so far away from her, turning to hurry back to the study. Work was always a good way to clear her mind, and she needed that more than anything now.

"Nora?"

Nora wiped the tears staining her cheeks away before turning around. Sally walked over to her and wrapped her arms around her.

"I'm sorry, Nora. I know you will miss him. I will miss him, too. He cared so much for you and was always so nice to me too. It will be hard without him here."

Nora couldn't stop the tears from flowing. She knew Sally understood. Nora had been happy, which made her sister happy. No matter how much her heart was breaking, Nora had to forget about Jack and move on. Crying on the job wouldn't be tolerated too well and she didn't want to raise any suspicions as to why she was crying, especially so close to Jack's departure.

"Thank you, Sally. He was special, wasn't he?"

Sally nodded. "Very."

"Sally, if I tell you something, promise me you will keep it secret forever?"

"Of course, Nora."

"Well, you remember how mother and father would tell us the story of their first kiss under mistletoe and how magical it was for them?"

"Yes, I loved that story, Nora. They said they knew they were meant to be together forever when they had their first kiss."

"Well, now I know how they felt, Sally. It's magical…"

Sally's mouth fell open. "What… what are you saying, Nora?"

"Well, I know for a fact that your first kiss with someone special, with someone who you really, really care about, can be magical, leave your heart racing a million beats a minute, and can make you realise how much you love someone."

Sally smiled. "You didn't… did you? Did you kiss Jack? And… you think you love him?!"

Nora nodded. "Yes, there was mistletoe hanging from the top of the door frame in the library. Oh, Sally, it was like I was dreaming. Jack came in, took my hand, had me close my eyes and led me over to the door. I saw this plant or something hanging down from the door frame. Jack leaned in; I got scared and stepped back…"

"You turned him down? Nora!!"

"No, I just got momentarily scared. He pulled me close again, and I didn't back away. Then… then he kissed me, Sally, and it was the most wonderful feeling I have ever felt in my life. His lips were warm and gentle, and I… I kissed him back. I really didn't know what I was doing but it felt natural and right."

Nora's cheeks reddened as she remembered the feel of Jack's lips on hers.

"Oh, that sounds wonderful, Nora. And you're sure no one saw you, right? Mr Bradley would be livid if…"

"Yes, I know. I was so lost in the moment that I forgot about where we were, and who we are – the merchant's son and the poor maid."

"Oh, Nora, why does life have to be like that? Why can't we just be with who we love? It's not our fault we aren't rich, Nora. We had a good life with mother and father, didn't we?"

"We absolutely did, Sally. But society doesn't see life how we see it. If we love someone, we should be able to love them without hiding it. But it would never work with Jack and me because of who he is – and who I'm not."

Sally didn't say anything, but Nora knew she understood. Life wasn't fair but at least Nora would have the memories of her and Jack's kiss in her heart forever.

"Oh, and after the kiss, Mr Bradley called out for his son! I was so scared he'd seen us but he hadn't. Jack stepped away from me and I ran, I mean I really ran, back to the books just in time to see Mr Bradley come in."

"I'm so glad, Nora. I don't even want to imagine what would have happened if he'd have caught you."

Nora felt her heart sink. She knew what would have happened to her, but she didn't want to voice those fears to Sally.

"Oh, I almost forgot. Jack had wanted to say something to me but then we heard Mr Bradley's voice calling for him so he couldn't talk anymore. And we never had time alone before he left."

Sally's face lit up. "I bet he was going to confess his feelings for you, Nora. I could see it in his face how he felt about you."

Nora shook her head. "I doubt that, Sally. He knows he could never be with me; his father would disown him. He probably just wanted to say an early goodbye to me. I'm sure it wasn't anything important."

"Sally?" Mrs Emsworth's voice rang out in the hallway. "Come help me with the laundry."

"Yes, Ma'am." Sally turned to Nora. "I don't know, Nora, but you're probably right. I want you to tell me more about the kiss when we're alone. Promise?"

Nora shook her head. "Absolutely. It feels so good to be able to talk to someone about this. And Sally, I never answered your question, but yes, I love him."

Nora didn't have time to think about Jack the rest of the day. She kept busy, re-dusting items she had previously dusted. The thoughts of their kiss kept playing in her head, making Nora smile for no reason at all. She hummed as she worked, remembering the first time she had met Jack. She didn't know then that he would become so special to her.

It was all worth it. She wouldn't trade all their talks, their closeness, their kiss, for anything. The sadness she felt at Jack leaving would fade with time, and she would have precious memories to comfort her throughout the years.

As Nora fell, exhausted, into bed that night she felt something beneath her head, inside the pillow. Thinking the pillow needed fluffing, she fluffed it, again and again, but it still felt uncomfortable to her. Her heartache came pouring out as she sat up in bed, grabbed her pillow and punched it – over and over again. The other girls didn't stir, and Nora was thankful that they were deep sleepers. She punched the pillow for what seemed like hours, relieving all her pent up feelings of Jack leaving.

When she lay back down, placing her head in the middle of the pillow, she felt the same uncomfortableness that wouldn't seem to go away. Thinking her pillow was old and worn out, she went to toss it onto the floor. That's when she noticed something was inside her pillow. Fearing a dead animal, although Nora knew the chance of a dead animal being inside her pillow was slim, she quietly crept out of the room, walking down the hall to where one single candle lit the hallway.

Holding the pillow beside the candle and getting down on her knees, she reached inside the pillow, holding her breath and waiting for her hand to touch something she really didn't want to touch.

She signed in relief when her hand felt a small piece of rolled up paper. Nora didn't know why or how paper had ended up inside her pillow, but she needed to get it out and dispose of it so she could get to sleep. The morning always came way too early, and Mrs Emsworth liked the girls downstairs bright and early. Too early for Nora's liking but such was her life now.

"Aha," she said out loud as she pulled the paper out. Holding it beside the candle, she could see writing on the paper. What was it? Had someone hidden something inside her pillow because they didn't want anyone else to see what they had written? Was someone trying to get her into trouble?

Her heart raced faster as her thoughts went out of control. Maybe Mr Bradley had seen her and Jack kiss and he was so livid with her that he didn't want to even talk to her to let her go. Maybe he'd written her a letter, stuffed it in her pillow case, so he didn't have to talk to her. He probably wanted her packed and gone by morning.

As panic overtook her, Nora refused to read what was on the paper. If Mr Bradley wanted her gone, well, he'd have to tell her face to face. With more energy than she felt, Nora tucked the paper into her pocket and quietly entered her room. With fear in her heart that she'd have to say goodbye to Sally in the morning, Nora slept very little, afraid that she'd never see Sally again.

***

Nora awoke, expecting to see her bag packed with a note asking that she leave. But there was nothing.

"Nora, you'd better get dressed. We have to be downstairs in less than 5 minutes."

Nora, confused, looked at Lucy. "Am I still here?"

All 3 girls looked at her. "What," they all said in unison.

"Of course you're still here, Nora. Where else would you be?" Sally looked concerned.

Nora laughed, trying to lighten the mood. "So sorry. I'm still half asleep. Of course I'm here. Okay, it'll just take me a minute to get dressed."

"You really have to get more sleep, Nora," Della said. "I hear you tossing and turning at night. If you get deprived of sleep, I've heard that can mess with your mind."

Nora nodded. She wished she could sleep like the girls did. As soon as their heads hit their pillows, they were asleep. But Nora had never been like that. Well, she had when she was little and her parents were there. But her life had changed for the worse once she'd lost them. Her life had had a small glimmer of happiness with Jack, but Nora knew that happiness was over, and she had to accept that Jack was gone.

Nora looked over her shoulder all day, waiting for Mr Bradley to appear and ask her why she was still there. She'd lie and say she had never seen his note. Which really wasn't a lie because she hadn't read his note. But he never appeared. As she started to relax, Mrs Emsworth called her into the kitchen.

This is it. Mr Bradley is having Mrs Emsworth let me go. He probably wanted to be sure I worked a full day before letting me go. What am I going to do? I can't leave Sally again; I promised her.

Her body visibly shaking, Nora walked into the kitchen, her eyes staring at her feet. How could they do this to her? It was just a kiss between her and Jack. That was it. Suddenly, Nora remembered what Mrs Emsworth had said about the former maid and the footman. Mrs Emsworth had made it very clear that Nora not partake in unladylike behaviour with a staff member. She could only imagine how livid Mrs Emsworth must be upon learning that Nora's unladylike behaviour was with Mr Bradley's son.

"Nora, look at me. Is everything all right?"

Nora looked up, expecting to see anger all over Mrs Emsworth's face. But there was none. Mrs Emsworth actually looked concerned for Nora's well-being as she looked at her.

"Yes, yes, Ma'am. Please, Mrs Emsworth, I can… let me tell you…" Nora stopped, not knowing what else to say. It was all her fault. Just like she had caused her dismissal from Lady Alva's home, she had caused her dismissal from Mr Bradley's home because she had kissed Jack. She had done it; Jack hadn't forced her. Now, she had to accept her punishment. Soon, she'd be gone. She prayed that Mr Bradley would let Sally stay.

"Okay, I'm glad to hear that, Nora." Mrs Emsworth interrupted Nora's thoughts.

Here it comes. I can handle it. There will be better things awaiting me.

"Can you help me with the dishes, Nora? I know you've been working very hard, but Mr Bradley insisted that his clothes be laundered, again, as he's leaving for a business trip tomorrow. I've assigned Della to the laundry and I've other tasks to attend to as well."

"Huh?" Nora didn't think she had heard Mrs Emsworth correctly. Why wasn't she being asked to pack her bags? Did Mr Bradley have a change of heart? Did Mrs Emsworth talk him into letting her stay?

"Can you help with the dishes, Nora?" Mrs Emsworth sounded annoyed this time.

For the first time since last night, Nora's heart stopped racing, and she felt herself calm down. She wasn't being escorted out. She could still work here. She could still be with Sally.

"Yes, Ma'am. Of course."

Mrs Emsworth shook her head in approval. "Good. Now get started; I have a million things to tend to and it's getting late into the evening."

As Nora finished the dishes and walked up the stairs to her room, she knew she had to read the letter. She was grateful that Mr Bradley had changed his mind and felt she could read the letter in peace.

While Nora wanted to read the letter while the other girls were discussing their day, she knew she couldn't. She didn't want any questions as to what she was reading. And if she was to be dismissed later, she didn't want to worry and upset Sally with that news.

It seemed like an eternity before the girls fell asleep. Getting out of bed as quietly as she could, she walked out into the hallway towards the single burning candle. With her hands shaking, she was barely able to open the rolled up piece of paper, but she managed to do it. Closing her eyes and willing her heart to stop racing, Nora gained her courage and looked down at the paper. The writing looked faint and she had to get closer to the candle in order to read it.

Nora,

I will miss you. I will be back. Please take care of yourself.

Jack

Nora felt the butterflies in her stomach; the same ones she felt when she was around Jack. He would miss her. He cared enough about her to leave her a note to let her know that. And he'd said he'd be back. That meant that she'd see him again, and that he wanted to see her again.

She broke down in laughter, letting all of her pent up fear escape. Mr Bradley hadn't seen their kiss; he wasn't angry with her and he didn't want her gone. She knew she needed to do better with her out of control thoughts, but her life had been nothing but heartache for so long that she always expected the worst. But now, now she could stop worrying. She was safe here; she was wanted here, and Jack said he would be back. Nora felt that her life was finally looking up and worth living to the fullest again.

Chapter 9

The weeks turned into months, and Nora struggled daily with thoughts of Jack. She missed him but she knew she had to keep her mind on her work or risk facing the wrath of Mrs Emsworth and Mr Bradley. Nora was good at keeping her struggles to herself, and not even Sally knew the emptiness and heartache she felt inside from missing Jack.

As spring turned into summer, Nora wondered what Jack was doing. Was he happy that it was summer and he had a break from his studies? Did he still miss her? Did he think about her? Her thoughts were always filled with the stolen times they'd had together, and she prayed that they would have many more in the future.

As Nora scrubbed the kitchen floor in mid-July, she heard footsteps walking down the hall. Fearing it was Mrs Emsworth checking on her, Nora scrubbed harder and faster. Her mind had wandered a bit, and she'd lost track of time. She should have moved on to her next task by now. Mrs Emsworth would surely offer a stern reprimand to her.

Nora didn't look up when she heard soft breathing behind her. She waited for Mrs Emsworth to ask her why scrubbing the kitchen floor was taking her so long, but she never heard those words.

"Nora..."

Her name was spoken as a whisper, and the familiar butterflies and quickened heartbeat returned as she recognised the voice. Jack. Jack was home.

She pretended not to hear. She didn't know what to say. She didn't feel as if she could stand up due to her body shaking uncontrollably. He hadn't let her down. He had come back, just as he had promised her.

"Nora, it's me. Jack."

She had to acknowledge him. Holding on to the scrub brush, she turned around slowly, her heart skipping a beat when she saw him. He looked even more handsome, if that was even possible.

She wanted to stand up, to hug him, to kiss him, but she knew her place. They could easily be caught, and the repercussions would be too high for both of them.

"Jack, hi," she spoke softly, her cheeks reddening as she held his gaze. Those eyes, those blue eyes that haunted her dreams each night.

"I told you I'd be back, Nora. I've thought about you often. I hope you are well. I hope you are happy."

I'm happy now that you are home, Jack. She knew she couldn't say those words out loud, even though she wanted to. "Yes, thank you, I am well."

Jack held her gaze before dropping his eyes. "I…I'm only home for a week; my father has some business items he wants to go over with me. Although I've just started at

University, he says it's time for me to learn the business." Jack looked defeated, and Nora knew he felt trapped. He had promised his father he would help him in his business, but Nora knew his heart's desire was not the business. Jack's fascination was in law, but he knew he must follow in his father's footsteps, so his interests had to be let go. While Nora understood, she was also sad to see Jack give up his passion in order to appease his father.

"I'm glad you're home," Nora said shyly, bringing a smile to Jack's face. "I…missed you." There she had said it.

"I missed you, as well, Nora. I know it sounds like a long time, Nora, but University is only four years. Then, I'll be around more, and well, we'll have more time to spend together."

No we won't. I'm tired of sneaking around. I don't want to be his hidden mistress, although I would never go that far with him. Oh why is this so complicated? Why can't I openly love him? Sneaking around feels awful to me; like I'm not worthy of being by his side openly. And four years? That is such a long time. What if Mr Bradley lets me go? Or Mrs Emsworth gets annoyed with me and puts me out on the streets? I'll never see him again.

"Yes." Nora had much more to say but she knew she couldn't. She knew she should listen to her thoughts and refuse to sneak around but her heart always overruled what her thoughts begged her to do. If she had to sneak around to be with Jack, she would do it. Even if she got caught and thrown out on the streets, she would have memories of someone that she loved; someone that cared about her. Sally would be fine without her. She'd soon be thirteen and could hold her own. Sally. She'd made a promise. Their lives were fairly good at the Bradley home. Why was she being stupid? Why was she willing to risk a good life with her sister by her side to sneak around with someone who wanted to keep her hidden? It made her feel dirty, like she wasn't worth anything to him. But her heart refused to listen to her head, and Nora knew she'd meet Jack whenever and wherever he wanted. She trusted him to keep her safe; trusted him to protect her if they were ever caught together.

That night, Nora met Jack in the library. He had whispered the time and place to her in passing and while Nora had wanted to say no, she found herself constantly checking the time, anticipating being alone with the boy she was in love with. Her bed creaked as she got up, and she sat there for a minute, making sure she hadn't woken the other girls up. Their soft breathing told her that she hadn't.

As she walked quietly down the stairs to the library, holding a candle to light her way, she had a moment of clarity which told her to go back to bed. But she couldn't. Her feet propelled her down the stairs, and she walked into the library, a candle illuminating Jack's features.

Nora sucked in a breath. He was handsome. He was kind. Why did he like her? What did he see in her?

"Nora, I thought you had changed your mind."

Nora saw his tense features relax as he smiled at her.

"I would never change my mind."

Nora stood frozen in place, not sure what to do.

Jack walked over to her, took her hand and led her to the chair by the desk. He set her candle on the desk, then sat down in the chair, pulling Nora into his lap. She felt the tension melt from her body as she relaxed against him. She felt safe with Jack.

"I've missed you so much, Nora. Our kiss, I've thought about that every day."

Nora gasped. He thought about that too? Was he telling her the truth? But why would he lie to her?

"I have too," she said shyly. "It… it was my first kiss, Jack."

Jack kissed her on the cheek. "I'm glad, Nora. I'm glad I was the first."

"Me too."

It only took a minute before Jack's lips touched hers. She kissed him back gently, wishing that time would stand still. As Jack pulled away, she laid her head on his chest, savouring the alone time and togetherness. They stayed there for ten minutes, until Jack told her that she'd better get back upstairs.

"Tomorrow night, here, same time?"

"Yes, Jack…"

With a soft kiss on Nora's forehead, Jack gripped her waist and helped her to her feet.

When he stood up, Nora hugged him, savouring the warmth of his arms around her. Sleep came late for her as she relived their kiss over and over again, until she fell asleep with a soft smile on her face.

Nora's humming brought a smile to Mrs Emsworth's face the next day.

"I'm glad you're enjoying your work, Nora. It's good to see you happy."

"Thank you, Mrs. Emsworth. I do enjoy my work."

Nora smiled. Her work seemed much more enjoyable now that Jack was home. She knew he'd be leaving soon, but she had no fear that he wouldn't come back to her. She knew he would. He'd come back for the holidays and maybe she could talk him into a summer visit. And in four years, he would be finished with University, and he would move back to the Bradley home. He'd be around more; Nora would see him more. That thought made her smile every time she thought about it. All she had to do was be respectful, work hard, and do a good job. Then she'd be kept on as a maid. Nora knew she could do that; she'd do it for Jack, and Sally. Maybe things would work out with Jack? Mr Bradley had become more cordial with the staff. Nora thought it was because of Jack. Jack was always friendly with the staff, and Nora knew he insisted his father show the staff more respect and stop being so brusque with them. Maybe, if Jack fell in love with her too, his father would want his son's happiness and wouldn't stand in their way. Maybe he would disregard society's opinion of him, of Jack, and let his son find happiness with her as Mr Bradley had done with Jack's mother.

Nora shook her head. Her heart was telling her silly thoughts again. Mr Bradley was cordial with the staff; that was all. He would never see her as anything but a maid; he would never allow his son to stoop that low and marry her. Although her head told her it could never be, she knew she'd follow her heart. With Jack, she'd always follow her heart, knowing full well heartbreak would probably creep in when Jack was finished with his studies. He'd enter his father's business, marry a wealthy girl, and Nora would continue on as a poor maid.

But she put those negative thoughts out of her head as she crept down the hallway holding her candle for the second night in a row. She was no longer afraid of being caught. Jack would never risk Nora being let go, and although the hour was late, it was the best time for them to be together. No one was up at that hour, and Nora felt sure that they were safe.

This time when Nora entered the library, she didn't stand still, frozen in fear. She boldly walked up closer to Jack, placed her candle on the desk and took his hand. With his other hand, Jack tilted her chin up and placed a kiss on her lips. When he pulled back and looked at Nora, she moved in closer, placed her hands on his cheeks and pulled him closer. This time, Nora kissed him, not caring about rules or etiquette or what Jack would think of such a brazen move from her. She just wanted to feel his warm lips on hers.

"Nora," Jack sounded breathless, "I care so much for you…"

Nora cut him off, placing a quick kiss on his lips. "And I do too. Care for you, I mean."

"Although I hate to say this, Nora, we must say goodnight. I will see you again tomorrow, if I may?"

"You may."

Nora and Jack met each night in the library, stealing sweet kisses until Jack had to return to University. While her heart broke when she saw him leave, she knew he'd be back for the holidays. Her fear of never seeing him again had been replaced with anticipation at seeing him again. She kept her spirits up over the next several months, and worked harder than she ever had.

Even though Nora had wanted to tell her sister about the stolen nights with Jack, she knew she needed to keep that secret to herself for now. There would be plenty of time to tell Sally later. She feared Sally would be upset with Nora for sneaking around in the middle of the night to see Jack, as Sally feared being separated from Nora. Nora felt it was best to keep her stolen moments with Jack to herself and not cause Sally any worry.

***

The holidays came faster than Nora was prepared for. The busy days and nights of preparing the Bradley home for the holidays had taken a toll on the girls.

Jack arrived three days before Christmas, and Nora hoped that Jack would want to spend time with her like they had in July, late at night in the library. Her prayers were answered when Jack found her alone in the parlour, tidying up the mess that Mr Bradley always seemed to make.

"Jack! I'm so glad you're home!"

"Nora, you look beautiful." Nora felt a blush creep onto her cheeks. "Shall we? The library at our usual time?"

"We shall," Nora smiled at him.

Jack took Nora's hand and kissed it. "Until then."

"Until then."

Nora got into the routine of working hard during the day and meeting Jack in the library at night. Those stolen minutes alone with him helped get her through the day. Mrs

Emsworth praised her work, and she noticed a few glares from the other girls. It was only because of Jack that Nora worked so hard. It was like she put her feelings for Jack into her work; and her love for Jack turned into excellent work around the Bradley home.

Being in Jack's arms, if only for a few minutes, became the highlight of Nora's day. She had come to realise that it didn't matter if he didn't love her; she knew he couldn't love her for she was not of his class, and that was not his fault. It was the family he was born into, and the family that she was born into. Nora knew he cared about her, and to her, that was as good as love. He respected her and was very kind to her; that was really all she needed, and wanted.

As the Christmas meal was prepared, Nora took extra care with the potatoes and vegetables that she was in charge of. She didn't want Jack, or Mr Bradley, to have a bad holiday meal. She hoped Jack would be impressed with her cooking, although she knew she wasn't the best cook. But if it was made with love, Nora knew it had to taste better.

When the staff was allowed their Christmas meal in their dining area, small handmade gifts were exchanged. Nora had bought Sally a small locket with their initials on the inside.

"Now you will always have a part of me next to your heart, Sally."

Sally had knitted Nora a blue hat. Sally had become a good knitter, and Nora envied her skill. "Thank you, it's beautiful, Sally."

Della and Lucy had given Sally and Nora small pins shaped like a flower, while the sisters gave the two girls silver hairpins. Nora's heart was full as the meal was finished and the clean-up began. There was just one more present Nora had to exchange, a present that she had hidden under her mattress, and one she could tell no one about.

As Nora entered the library that night, she worried that Jack might not like her gift. It had cost her several weeks' pay but she thought it would be perfect for him. She'd wrapped it in newspaper as that was all she could find.

"Hello, Nora. Merry Christmas."

"Merry Christmas, Jack."

Jack walked over to her and gave her a kiss on her forehead before holding out a small box to her. "I hope you like it."

"I know I will. For you," she said shyly, holding up the newspaper wrapped gift.

"Thank you, Nora, but you didn't have to."

"I know I didn't Jack but I wanted to. I always felt bad that I didn't give you anything last year, our first Christmas together."

"But I didn't get you anything either, Nora. I didn't know if you would have found it inappropriate or not as we were just getting to know each other at that time."

"That's fine, Jack. Spending time with you, talking with you, last year was the best present you could have given me. Now should I open my gift first or do you want to?"

"You go first, Nora."

With shaking hands, Nora opened the elegantly wrapped box. She felt ashamed that his gift was wrapped in newspaper, but it was all that she had.

"Jack…it's…they're beautiful."

"I hope you like them, Nora."

"Oh I do."

Inside the small box were the prettiest blue-coloured earrings that Nora had ever seen. And they were heart shaped. "I love them, Jack. They're beautiful. And they're the colour of your eyes." Nora blushed at what she had just said, but Jack didn't say anything.

"Now, open yours, Jack."

Jack ripped the newspaper wrapping off and took the lid off of the small box. He removed the handkerchief and held it up, a smile forming on his lips.

"Thank you, Nora."

"Look at the bottom right corner, Jack."

Jack opened the handkerchief, his eyes resting at the bottom right. "J + N".

"Jack plus Nora," she said.

"Yes, I know."

When his eyes locked with hers, Nora felt dizzy. He always did this to her. He made her heart beat fast and her world spin. He made her feel so alive in ways that she never dreamt possible.

Their kiss lasted longer than the others had. They clung to each other, basking in love. At least, it was love to Nora. The night had been magical. Nora held the small box holding her earrings close to her as she walked up the stairs to her room. She would treasure this night, and her gift, forever.

Chapter 10

Jack's return to University had been filled with thoughts of Nora. Their stolen kisses, their special time together. He was seventeen now; Nora was fifteen. He had never met a girl like Nora. She was beautiful, caring and kind. He knew she worked hard, and he saw how well she got along with everyone. She'd even managed to charm his father a bit.

His father. Ever since his mother had passed, his father had turned into a person that Jack no longer recognised. It was as if his father cared only about money now. He'd talked to his father about showing the staff a bit more respect instead of raising his voice to them and threatening to turn them out on the streets if he felt their work wasn't up to his standards. His father was now a bit more cordial to them; which Jack was happy to accept.

Jack focused hard on his studies, and excelled at University. He thought about Nora, every day. He always had the handkerchief with him and looked often at "J + N." It kept him going at school. Nora was the reason he focused so hard on his studies; he wanted her to be proud of him. He wanted her to see that he could provide a good future for them.

Jack knew he didn't want a future without Nora in it. He'd felt an immediate attraction to her from the first time he saw her. It was like a punch in his gut. He remembered his father telling him that he felt he'd been knocked off his feet the first time he'd seen his mother. Now, Jack knew what his father had experienced when he'd first met his mother.

Christmas time was the highlight of Jack's year. Seeing Nora, being around her and feeling her soft lips on his, were what he looked forward to. Time always went too slow at University; it seemed to take forever until the holiday break arrived. But holiday break always went too fast; his time with Nora always went too fast, and then he'd be back at University, with only thoughts of her to get him through the rest of the school year.

While Jack had never wanted to return home to the Bradley home during summer break, he found himself going home for two weeks every July. While he told his father he'd come home to learn more about the business and to assist him in it, the real reason for going home was Nora.

Nights in the library in each other's arms, sweet kisses, and sharing their hopes and dreams for the future were the only reason he chose to go home. Two weeks always went by too fast, and he'd have five long months before he would see Nora again.

University would be over one day, and Jack knew what he would do. He would ask Nora to be his wife. His father would accept it or he wouldn't. It wasn't his father's life he had to live; it was his own life. Jack knew the love his father had felt for his mother; surely, he would understand Jack's love for Nora.

***

"You're eighteen, Nora!" Sally beamed with pride at her sister. "You're all grown up. And you're so beautiful."

"Eighteen, yes. But beautiful…I don't think so…"

"Oh stop, you know you are," Lucy teased. "Happy birthday, Nora."

"We baked you a cake!" Sally said. "We even got a little help from Mrs Emsworth. After all, it's not every day you turn eighteen!"

As the staff celebrated Nora's day with her favourite cake, she reflected how far she and Sally had come. The years at the Bradley house had been good for them. Their lives weren't always easy; they worked hard and were paid much less than they should have been; but they'd been together. And that was all that mattered to Nora.

Jack had come home every holiday and two weeks every summer. They'd had their alone time each night he was home in the library. His kisses and embraces made her feel like he really did love her, although he had never spoken those words. Nora had wanted to but she kept the words in her heart. She was sure her actions and her eyes reflected her love for him, but if he knew how she felt, he never mentioned it.

Nora would go to bed each night dreaming of the next time she would see him. Twice a year was never enough, but she looked forward to Jack's return home. She knew his studies at University were going well, and she told him how proud she was of him. Time had seemed to pass much too slowly in the four years that she had known Jack, especially since they only had several weeks to spend together each year. But now, Jack was graduating University and would soon be back in the Bradley home. She'd see him almost every day; except when he had to travel with his father for business. But that would be short lived. He'd never be gone for long months at a time again.

"Jack will be home soon!" Sally whispered when they had a few minutes alone.

"I know; I'm so excited to see him, Sally."

Nora had only recently told Sally about all the secret meetings she'd had with Jack over the years. Although Sally was shocked, she was very happy for Nora.

"I know how much you love him, Nora. What do you think will happen when he graduates University? Do you think there would ever be a chance that you could be together? Like in marriage?"

Nora shook her head. "No. I don't think Mr Bradley would ever agree to that. Jack would have to leave here; leave the business."

"Do you think he would?"

"I'd like to think so, but I don't know, Sally. Why would he want to give up his secure future for me? It wouldn't make sense."

"Has he told you he loves you?"

"No."

"Have you told him?"

"No."

"Exactly."

Nora looked at her sister. "Exactly? What do you mean?"

"You love him and haven't told him. I see the way you look at him. I see that same way he looks at you. I know he loves you, too. So, he loves you and hasn't told you because you haven't told him."

Nora laughed. "How did you get so grown up?"

"Turning sixteen will do that to you."

The girls laughed.

"Well, we'd better get back to work before Mrs Emsworth sees us laughing and thinks we're up to something. Happy birthday again, Nora."

As Sally walked away, Nora thought about what Sally had said. Could Jack possibly love her too? She shook her head. But what good would ever come of it? Sally was probably imagining what she had seen on Jack's face when he was with Nora. And that was definitely for the best.

***

Christmas went by faster than any other Christmas. Jack would be done with University in a few months, and Nora looked forward to having him home. She knew the next several months would go slow, but then,

Jack would be home for good. They wouldn't have to be separated again.

As they spent their last night together in the library, Jack pulled Nora onto his lap. They sat in silence for several minutes, savouring their last moments together before Jack went back to University.

"Nora," Jack broke the silence. "You know I care about you so much…"

"Yes, I know, Jack."

"But… it's…it's much more than that, Nora. I…love you."

Nora's heart dropped. Did he just say that he loved her? Had she imagined it?

"Huh?" was all that Nora could get out. She prayed that he would repeat those words.

Then she'd truly know what he'd just said; she'd know she hadn't imagined it.

"I love you, Nora. Always have. For four years, I've known. If you don't feel the same way, I'll understand. But I couldn't keep it in any longer. I wanted you to know."

"I love you, too, Jack. I have for a long time, too."

They held each other and sat in silence.

"Nora, I'll be out of University soon. I'll be home; we'll be together. No more sneaking around, I promise. I… I want you to be my wife, Nora. We can get married over the summer, whether I have my father's blessing or not. My father should understand how I feel, Nora, as he had the same feelings for my mother."

"Wife? Oh, Jack, you want to… marry me?"

"I never want to be separated from you again, Nora. I'll provide a good life for you. And for Sally."

"Yes, Jack. Yes! I would love to be your wife. It's all I've ever wanted… But what if your father doesn't approve?"

"We'll figure it out, Nora. There will be other options for me than eventually taking over my father's business. It will be okay, Nora. I'll be talking to him tonight or tomorrow before I go back to University. It's time he knows the truth."

"But what… what if he turns me out, Jack? Maybe you should wait…"

"He won't Nora. I'll make him promise me he won't do anything until I'm home. It's only a few months, Nora."

Nora felt her heart sink but she had to trust Jack; she had to trust that he'd make sure she had a roof over her head until he came home.

***

"No son of mine is marrying a maid! How will that look to others? You'll make me look like a fool, Jack, and I will not stand for that. Can you imagine the looks I'll get? The comments behind my back about Jack Bradley marrying a lowly servant? I will not permit this, Jack. We had an agreement. You finish University and help me in the business with the intention that you will take over the business when I get older. This could ruin us.

This could ruin the business. Do you want to be out on the streets? Do you want to be working as a footman in a neighbour's house? Think about what you're doing, Jack!"

"If I'm on the streets, so be it. Why should who I fall in love with, who I marry, matter to the people we do business with? Why would our neighbours care? It's MY life, Father, not yours. I'm marrying Nora, not you. I'll pursue another career; you know I've always wished to work in law; I've never wanted to work as a merchant. I was just honouring what you wanted for me, but I'm not a child anymore. I can make my own decisions. Nora and I will be married this summer. We will find our own place to live. All I ask is that you allow her to continue to work here until I come home. Then, we'll be gone. I won't ever bother you again."

"I won't ever accept this, Jack. I won't have you making me look like a fool and ruin a business I've spent years building up. Once you graduate, you'll come home, pack your belongings and take that maid with you."

As his father stormed out of the room, Jack took several deep breaths to calm his racing heart. While he'd expected his father to be upset at the news, he never expected it would be that bad. His father had just disowned him. While Jack felt a sadness, he also felt relief. His father had turned into a man Jack never wanted to become. He'd make a good life for Nora and Sally away from here. His father would come to regret pushing his only child out of his life forever.

***

Nora awoke the next morning, getting dressed quickly in order to see Jack off. When she entered the kitchen, Mrs Emsworth instructed her to clean up the dining table and wash the dishes.

"Jack left early this morning," Mrs Emsworth said to Nora, "That's why there's dishes already. Mr Bradley told me last night to prepare a good meal for him as he had to leave for University earlier than he normally did."

While Nora was disappointed that she wouldn't get to see Jack before he left; she understood that plans had to change at times. She prayed that he'd have a safe journey back to University. She was going to tell Sally that evening about Jack wanting to make her his wife, and that he had promised to make a good life for the two of them.

"Nora, come with me," Mrs Emsworth sounded irritated as she stepped into the parlour where Nora was cleaning.

Nora stopped dusting, set her rag down, and followed Mrs Emsworth into the study. Several long minutes later, Mr Bradley came in, slamming the door so hard that a book fell off of the desk.

Nora was terrified. She knew Jack had mentioned speaking to his father last night but she didn't know if he had. Was something wrong?

"I'm letting you go, Nora. Your work has become below my standards, and I'm missing money that I had stored in a box in here. Since you are the one who is in here the most, it's you who is the thief. I won't have thieves in my home. Mrs Emsworth, escort this thief upstairs while she packs, then show her the door. She's not welcome here anymore."

Nora's heart hit the floor. *This can't be happening! I'm not a thief. I didn't steal money.*

"Mr Bradley, please, I…I didn't take money. I would never steal from you. I don't know what box you are referring to. Please, Mr Bradley. I'll do anything; I'll work harder. You don't even have to pay me. I have nowhere to go…"

"You should have thought about that before you stole. I have nothing more to say to you. And I will not give you a reference, at least not a good one."

Mrs Emsworth looked at Nora with shock and disgust. "How could you do that, Nora? You had a good life here. Your sister is here. I have to admit, I never thought of you as a thief, but I've been fooled before. Now let's go."

Mrs Emsworth motioned with her hand for Nora to go ahead of her. "Let's get you packed and out of here before Mr Bradley returns."

"Nora, what is wrong? Did something happen?" A worried Sally ran to her sister's side, following Nora and Mrs Emsworth up the steps.

"Sally, get back to your chores," Mrs Emsworth stated.

"I will not. Not until I hear what is going on."

"I've been let go, Sally."

"She's a thief is what she is," Mrs Emsworth spat out. "Mr Bradley has turned her out. She is to pack and leave immediately."

"Well, if Nora is going, so am I," Sally was adamant. "I'll get my bag packed as well."

Mrs Emsworth stood outside of the room while Nora packed. She knew Mr Bradley was lying. She knew that no money was stolen. The real reason she was being turned out was because of Jack. She knew that Jack had spoken to his father and he had not taken the news well. She knew he would not let his son marry a maid.

Nora whispered to Sally everything as fast as she could. She told her that Jack wanted to marry her, that Jack had spoken to his father, and was sent back to University early that morning. She told Sally she didn't steal anything and she believed the real reason she was let go was because Mr Bradley didn't want his son to be around her. Ever.

"I'm going with you," Sally whispered.

"No, you're not. You're sixteen. You have a roof over your head and a safe place to live. I'll be fine, Sally. You have to trust me. I can take care of myself. I will come back for you once I'm settled, but please, work hard and keep to yourself. I could never live with myself if he were to turn you out, too."

"I will stay only because you want me to, Nora. But I shall be worried every day until I see you again. Will you go back to the workhouse? I know it's horrid but at least you won't be on the streets."

"I most likely will," Nora lied. She didn't want to tell Sally that she'd never go to that awful place again because she didn't want her sister worrying about her.

"Let's go, thief girl," Mrs Emsworth called out.

"I'll be back soon, Sally. I promise."

Chapter 11

Nora stood outside the Bradley house, too shocked to move. How had her life gone from magical to ruined in a few minutes? She blamed herself. She shouldn't have told Jack that she loved him. She should have kept that a secret from him. If she hadn't agreed to be his wife, Jack wouldn't have gone to his father. And she wouldn't be where she was now, lonely and scared, with nowhere to go.

She prayed that she would find work. Perhaps she should return to Lady Alva's and beg for forgiveness. But if Lady Alva rejected her, then what would she do?

This was all her doing; if she hadn't confessed her love; she'd still be inside. With Sally. With a warm place to sleep.

She had only meagre wages with her; they wouldn't last long. She needed to find a place to sleep. She could go a few days without food; perhaps she would find work by then.

She found a corner in an alley by a tenement building to sleep her first night out on the streets. She was terrified to close her eyes, but sleep overcame her. When she woke as the sun began to rise, she looked around, confused. Where was she? Then the horrid memories of the day before came flooding back. She was alone now; she had no one. Jack would not know that Nora had been let go. Not until he came home, close to five long months.

She had to survive. She had to get through the next five months. She'd promised Sally she'd come back for her. She had to get settled. She was a good worker, surely someone would give her a chance and take her in as a maid? That thought momentarily gave Nora hope. She would find work.

After three days of going door to door at the grand houses many blocks from the corner where she slept, Nora was unable to find work. As she approached the seventh house and knocked on the door, she prayed her luck would change. Surely, someone would want her? She'd work hard and not be a problem.

"Yes?" an older woman looked her coldly up and down.

"Hello, Ma'am. I… I'm looking for work. As a maid or cook or anything…"

"You look like you haven't bathed or had a decent meal in some time," the woman said, shaking her head.

"No Ma'am."

"Have you worked as a maid before?"

"Yes, Ma'am. I worked at the Bradley home for years."

"Oscar Bradley? YOU worked for him?"

"Yes, Ma'am. Until several days ago. Please, Ma'am I'm a hard worker."

"I'm happy to take a look at your reference from Mr Bradley."

"I don't have one, Ma'am. Please, can you just give me a chance?"

"I'm afraid not, Miss. You stink to high heaven and I'm not sure I believe your story of working for Mr Bradley. Now off you go."

Nora had the seventh door slammed in her face.

As she spent another cold night huddled in the alley of the tenement building clutching her small bag tightly, the tears came. And she couldn't get them to stop.

Out of desperation, Nora approached the workhouse. She was tired of living on the streets. She was terrified at night. She knew if she didn't find a safe place at night, something bad would happen. She felt it in her soul.

She hung her head and knocked on the door. She was ready to face the matron's wrath. She'd beg to be taken back. She'd work 20 hours a day if she had to.

"We're full," a man said, not even looking at her.

At least it wasn't the matron. "Sir, please, I've been here before. I worked as a maid for Mr Bradley until several days ago. Please, I'm a hard worker. I have nowhere else to go."

The man still didn't look at her. He looked at her ragged clothes and shoes. "Like I said, we're full."

On day eight, Nora approached several shops in town but was told there was no work. "Please, I'll work for half wage. I'll work long days, I have nothing. Can't you please help me?"

The woman actually looked sorry for Nora, but still shook her head. "I'm afraid I can't, Miss. We can't afford to take on any more workers. I am sorry."

Nora nodded and turned to walk away.

"Miss?"

Nora turned around. Perhaps she had changed her mind.

"Here. Take these biscuits; you look like you haven't eaten in weeks."

Disappointed that the woman had not changed her mind about work, Nora took the biscuits, grateful to have something to eat. She'd foraged through dumpsters, eating any scraps of food she could find. But it wasn't enough. She knew she'd lost weight as her clothes hung off of her.

Days turned into months. Nora had started begging for food or money. When she received nothing for the day, she got her food from the dumpsters. It sustained her but her spirits were low. She didn't know how much longer she could survive. She'd befriended a young woman, not much older than herself, on the streets, and they had found an uninhabited building to spend their nights in. Although it was better than sleeping in alleyways, the rats and insects that ran through the building terrified Nora.

It was now April, but her threadbare shawl was not enough to keep her warm, even though the weather had turned milder. She prayed that she would find work and safer shelter soon before spring, then summer, turned into fall and winter. The only consoling thought she had at night was that Sally was in a safe place with a roof over her head.

One day when Nora was leaving the factory, after being told there was no work there, two men approached her. Nora was immediately on guard and clutched her bag tightly to her chest. She put her head down, planning to hurry past them. But one of the men roughly grabbed her, dragging her several feet before Nora was able to kick him and break free. She knew what they wanted – to kidnap her and force her into prostitution. She would die first before she let that happen to her, and the strength in which she fought off the men came from that thought. If she died fighting, well that was better than having to sell her body for a bit of coin.

"We have a feisty one, don't we?" the other man said. "Don't think you're getting away, lady. Because you ain't."

Not looking back, Nora ran, fearing they would overpower her and this time, she would lose. She had no more fight left in her. She ran inside a tavern, ducking behind the bar, to the surprise of the middle-aged man standing behind it.

"Whoa, Miss, what are you doing? You came barrelling in here like a horse that got frightened and ran off."

Nora didn't say anything. She was still shaking from her run in with the men.

"Miss? You'll have to leave."

"I'm sorry, Sir, I was just attacked. I broke free and ran in here so they wouldn't try to…"

The man just looked at her. "Calm down, Miss. Now come out from under the bar."

Nora stood up and walked to the front of the bar where she could see the man looking her up and down. Nora turned to run away but the man grabbed her arm. "Well, well, no wonder those men wanted you, you're a pretty young thing. I bet you clean up real well."

"Let go of me you…" She dropped her bag trying to wrangle free of his grip.

"Calm down, Missy. I meant you no harm. You looking for work?"

Nora stared at him. "I'm not that kind of girl, Mister, and you better let go of my arm or else…"

The man let her go and laughed. "I don't run a prostitution business here Missy if that's what you're thinking. I have a respectable tavern…"

"I bet."

"Look, we could use some help here. A barmaid You won't have to do anything beyond that, if you understand what I mean."

Nora nodded. She understood.

"The wage is low but I'll also give you one meal a day. By the looks of you, you look like you could use one. You have a place you're living?"

Nora nodded. "Sort of but… well, it's not nice…"

"There's an attic up there," he pointed towards the ceiling. "There's not a lot of space but you can sleep there if you need to."

Nora stood silent for several minutes. Working as a barmaid wasn't something she wanted to do. But she had nothing else. She'd gone three months begging for money and food, and sleeping in alleyways and rat infested buildings. She had no choice as to what she should say.

"Yes, thank you. When can I start?"

"Do you need to go get your things?" he asked, looking at the small bag she carried.

"No, Sir. I have all my possessions with me."

"Right. Now come with me. Get yourself washed and cleaned up." He walked over to a small closet to his right. "Here, put this on when you're done and come back down. We're set to have a busy day."

Nora fell down on her knees in the cramped attic, her back hurting and her spirit broken. Her first day as a barmaid had been horrid. Having to fend off several unwanted advances from the tavern's rough customers had terrified her. She felt her safety was in danger if she turned them down; but she'd never sink so low as to sell her body. She shivered at the thought. Too exhausted to cry, Nora lay on her side, willing herself to fall asleep. While she was grateful she'd have a roof over her head and food in her belly, that was all she could be grateful for at the moment. Her life was a living hell, and Nora saw no way to escape it.

Chapter 12

Jack paced in his room at University. He'd sent Nora two letters and had not received a reply back. The first he'd sent two months ago. He waited a month before sending the second one. Had she changed her mind about marrying him? Had she ever really loved him? Or had she told him she loved him only because he had told her first?

In his soul, he felt that something was wrong. Perhaps the first letter had been lost along the way. Maybe it was delivered to the wrong household. Maybe she'd misplaced it or forgot to write back to him. But the second letter? He failed to believe that the second letter was lost, or misplaced. A million thoughts were going through Jack's mind. He refused to shake off the thought that she didn't want to marry him anymore. If she'd changed her mind, he wanted to hear that from her. After all that they had shared over the years, she at least owed him a chance to find out what happened. If she had fallen out of love with him, he needed to hear that.

***

"Where is she?" Jack stormed into his father's study, startling the man as he was looking at papers on his desk.

"And who is 'she'?" Mr Bradley asked. "And what are you doing home?"

"That doesn't matter. Nora. Where is Nora?"

"Oh, the maid? Is that who you're referring to?"

"Where is she, Father?"

"She left not long after you returned to University. She left for a new job. I have no idea where she went as she did not leave a forwarding address."

Jack felt his heart breaking. That was why Nora hadn't replied. She had left and had never received his letter. But why? Why would she leave so soon after he went back to school? Why wouldn't she let someone know where she was going? Jack could only surmise that she'd left because of him. She didn't want to marry him and was too afraid to tell him, so she left.

Didn't she know how this would crush me? Why couldn't she have been honest with me?

After several agonising hours of pacing in the gardens, Jack felt it hard to believe that Nora had suddenly secured a new job and left suddenly without leaving a forwarding address. She had promised him she'd continue working for his father until he graduated from University. Nora wasn't one to break a promise. She hadn't even mentioned to him that she was looking for other work. He knew in his heart that she wouldn't leave without telling him goodbye or offering him any sort of explanation.

He approached Della and Lucy first, but they seemed sincere when they told him that they did not know what happened to Nora.

She had worked that morning and then they hadn't seen her anymore. When they went back to their room that night, Nora was missing. All Sally had told them was that Nora had to go.

"Had to go? Did Sally say why… or where?"

But Della and Lucy had nothing more to tell him.

Jack was shocked, either they were lying to him, or they really didn't know what happened to Nora. And wouldn't she have told them if she was leaving for a new job? Jack believed that Nora would have.

He found Sally in the library, dusting off books. "Sally?"

Sally, startled, dropped her rag, turning around to see who had called her name.

"Jack? Jack! What are you doing home?"

"Where's Nora, Sally? Did something happen?"

"Sally, get back to work." Mrs Emsworth's face peeked around the door frame.

"She will in a moment, Mrs Emsworth. But for now, please give us some time."

Mrs Emsworth shook her head. "Very well, but your father won't be as easy to shoo away."

"I'll deal with him. Now please, go."

"Oh, Jack, it was awful. Nora told me that Mr Bradley accused her of stealing. He said there was some box in the study that he kept money in and he accused Nora of taking it. She would never do such a thing. You have to believe that, Jack. Nora is not a thief. She's a hard worker and would never steal."

Jack was at a loss for words. His father had accused the woman he loved of stealing from him? And what box in the study was he talking about? He knew his father would never keep money in some imaginary box in the study.

"Jack? Are you listening?"

"Yes, go on."

"So Mrs Emsworth escorted Nora upstairs so she could pack her bag. I told Nora I was going with her but she told me to stay here and she'd be back for me when she was settled. But it's been close to four months now, Jack. I'm afraid something has happened to her."

Almost four months? She had been gone for four months? Panic rose up in him, and he felt sick to his stomach. Anything could have happened to her. He tried to calm his thoughts, rationalising that she probably had found a job and had a roof over her head. But if she hadn't? Jack didn't want to think about that.

"Sally, I had no idea. I had no idea my father would do such a nasty thing. This is all my fault. I spoke to him the night before I went back to University and told him I intended to marry your sister. And he didn't take it well. But I never thought he'd turn

Nora out. Never. If I'd have had any idea, I wouldn't have left."

"It's not your fault, Jack," Sally said softly. "You love her, you didn't turn her out."

Jack shook his head, but he did blame himself. He should have known his father would take his anger out on Nora. But it was his father, and he wanted to believe he could trust him.

Jack couldn't control his anger as he stormed back into his father's study.

"So you threw her out? You lied and accused her of stealing from you. Some imaginary box with money in your study. You know as well as I do that there is no box with money in here, and you also know that Nora didn't steal anything! She would never do such a thing."

"You need to lower your voice, Jack. I will not tolerate such blatant disrespect from you."

"Disrespect? After what you've done? You knew I loved her, Father. I told you I did. I told you I intended to marry her and all you cared about was your reputation and your money. You didn't…don't… care about your son. Your one and only child! What has happened to you?"

"That's enough!" Mr Bradley stood up and slammed his fist on his desk. "Get out of here, NOW."

"I will not, Father. I will not back down this time. This time, you've gone too far. I've watched you go from a loving father before we lost Mother to a horrid monster who only cares about his almighty money. You don't care about your own flesh and blood. I was crushed when we lost Mother. I loved her very much, like you did. You turned into this horrid human being once she was gone. I didn't know you anymore. I thought it was grief and that you'd go back to the man I admired above everything else in this world, but that never happened. You got nastier and nastier…"

"I said ENOUGH!"

"You will hear me out, Father, and then I will leave. And I will not be back."

Mr Bradley walked over to the window, standing in silence while he watched the sun light up the gardens.

"When I lost Mother, I lost my father, too." Jack stopped, the heartache from all the years of feeling unloved rising up in his soul. "And I've never gotten my father back. You know how I feel. You loved Mother more than your own life; that is how I feel about Nora. Would you have walked away if Grandfather had forbid you to marry Mother? Would you have?"

Mr Bradley stood in silence for several minutes before answering. "No. No I would not have walked away."

"And would you have searched the ends of the earth for her if she had been sent away on a lie? For something she didn't do?"

"Yes, I would have. I would have searched until my dying day to find her."

"And then you have some idea of how I'm feeling right now. You know what I have to do. So help me, Father, she better still be alive out there somewhere or you will lose the only flesh and blood who somehow still cares for you."

Jack and Mr Bradley stood in silence as the minutes went by. Jack had said all he'd needed to say.

"Money," Jack broke his silence. "I need money to find Nora and so I have a place to stay as I won't be staying here. That's the least you can do for me as I try to rectify this horrid mess you've made. And Sally better be here when I come back. Don't you dare do to her what you've done to Nora."

***

"Sally, I'm going to find her. And I will find her."

"I'm coming with you."

"No, you're not."

"Please, Jack. Your father could turn me out like he did Nora…"

Jack tried to reassure Sally. "No, he won't Sally. You have to trust me. You'll be safe here. Soon, you'll come with Nora and me after we're married. I'll make sure you have a good life, Sally. But for now, you need to stay here."

"Leaving already, Jack?" Mrs Emsworth called out as he walked by the kitchen.

Jack had no respect for the woman anymore. She'd been the one who'd escorted

Nora to the door. He'd known her all his life and had never known her to be so cruel.

"Yes, I am. I'm going to find Nora. You remember her don't you, Mrs Emsworth. Nora, who you called "thief girl" and escorted her out the door? And God knows where she is now because of you and my father!"

Mrs Emsworth looked at the floor. "Jack, I was just doing what your father told me to do. He said she'd stolen money. Why was I not to believe him?"

Jack laughed. "Why shouldn't you believe him? Have you EVER seen a box in the study? Did you EVER know my father to keep money around the house, especially in the study where the maids are in and out of? Have you?"

"I can't say I recall the box, Jack, but I wasn't sure…"

"What has happened to my father, Mrs Emsworth? He's a horrid representative of who he used to be when my Mother was alive. My Mother treated you as a sister, Mrs Emsworth; she treated the young staff as her children. What has happened to my home?"

"I'm sorry, Jack, I had no choice…"

"Do you know the real reason he let Nora go? Because I love her. Because I told my father I was going to marry her. And he was angry about that. So he took it out on Nora. And you know the rest."

Jack could tell by the look on Mrs Emsworth's face that she'd only just now found out the real reason for Nora's dismissal.

Jack hoped the guilt in the part that she played, and calling Nora a thief, would keep her up at night. That would be a small price to pay for whatever Nora was going through.

***

Two weeks had passed and Jack had not located Nora. He'd walked the streets day and night, stopping in shops, in factories and even the workhouse but she was nowhere. He refused to think that she'd been kidnapped and forced into prostitution. He knew Nora had a fighting spirit, and she would fight to the death to avoid a life like that.

After one more week of not finding her, he began to give up hope. With his heart sinking and almost out of money, he knew he had to return to University. He needed to take his final examinations so he could graduate.

Once exams were over, he would be free to search for Nora as long as he needed to until he found her.

"Jack! Did you find her?" Sally looked hopeful as she looked at the door behind Jack, expecting Nora to walk in behind him.

"No, Sally, I haven't."

The look of shock on Sally's face was how Jack felt. Three long weeks of walking streets with rough men and prostitutes propositioning him had been for naught. Nora was nowhere to be found.

"Are you going to look for her again? If you're not, I will…"

"Yes, I will. I have to go back to University but it's only for one week, Sally. I will graduate and come back. And then I will search for your sister until I find her. Please write to me if you hear anything, Sally. I'll drop everything and come back here. But you will see me in one week, okay?"

Sally shook her head. One more week without her sister in whatever horrid conditions she was living in.

Chapter 13

Nora had finally written a letter to Sally. She knew she should have written sooner but her work was exhausting and she'd received no wages from her work. Mr Johnson had told her he couldn't afford to pay her after all, and she should be thankful she had a good hot meal a day and a roof over her head. When she'd asked him for a stamp he grudgingly handed one over to her, and she'd gotten the letter off.

She knew Sally would be relieved to hear that she was all right after so much time had passed. She wasn't entirely truthful with Sally about her job as she didn't want her sister to worry about her. She'd told Sally she hoped to see her soon, although she didn't know how she would see her unless she snuck to the Bradley estate late at night when no one would see her.

Mr Johnson had turned into a somewhat fatherly figure to Nora, threatening the men in the tavern who tried to pull Nora onto their laps or touch her body. While it worked on most men, some threatened Mr Johnson, and Nora was left fighting them off when they tried to touch her. She knew she needed to leave the tavern but the thought of trying to find work elsewhere made her sick. What if she couldn't find anything else or found work that was worse than being a barmaid?

Her nights were filled with thoughts of Jack, and her dreams were filled with the happy life they'd live after they got married.

But she knew her dreams would never become a reality. This was her life now; she'd never see Jack again. And even if she did, would he still want her? Would he still love her?

***

The week at University was the longest week of Jack's life. He'd done well on his exams and had graduated at the top of his class. This should have been a happy time for him. He should be going home and planning a wedding with Nora. Now, she was gone. All because of his father's lies. But now, he had time. He had all the time in the world to find the woman he loved. His father had given him money the first time he'd searched for Nora; he'd have to give Jack more now. And more. Until he found her.

***

"Jack, you're back!" Sally rushed over to give him a hug. "I got a letter from Nora. It came the day after you left. Here." She pulled the letter out of her pocket and handed it to Jack. "She's working in a factory. She says it's hard work but she's earning a wage and has a safe place to stay at night."

Jack read the letter, relieved that Nora was alive and safe. "Can you make out the return address, Sally?"

"It looks like Lycher Street but I'm not sure."

Jack felt fear rise up again. The street address was almost illegible but he hoped it wasn't Lycher Street. It was full of the roughest men and women in London. And he didn't know of any factories there.

"Could it be Blyler Street?"

Sally looked at the letter again. "Perhaps it could be…"

Blyler Street had two factories located along its stretch, and it wasn't as dangerous as the area Lycher Street was in.

"Are you going to unpack, Jack? Can I come with you to find her?"

"I won't be staying here, Sally. Let's just say my father and I need a break. I just came here to get a few things. And no, you stay here young lady. When I find her, I'll let you know."

Although Sally was disappointed, she shook her head. She prayed that she'd see her sister soon.

Jack found his father in the library, leafing through a book. "Hello, Father, I'm not staying but I need money to rent an apartment in a bachelor establishment."

"You know, you can stay here, Jack…"

"I don't want to. So if you will…"

"Look son, I'm sorry. I'm sorry for all that's happened. I hope you can one day forgive me."

Jack stared at his father in silence. "I don't know, Father. That will depend on when, and if, I find Nora. You'll never be able to make up for what you did to her, Father."

Mr Bradley nodded. "I can't change the past, Jack, but I can hopefully give you, and Nora, a secure future."

Jack walked up Blyler Street, stopping into the factories and shops, searching for Nora. No one knew of a girl named Nora. Even when he described her, they shook their heads. It was like she had vanished. One letter to her sister months after she'd left, and it seemed like she no longer existed.

On day three, Jack abandoned Blyler Street, a sinking feeling in his stomach as he walked toward Lycher Street. But why would Nora be there? It was two miles from Blyler Street where the factories were located.

Prostitutes with over-painted faces offered him a cheap price for an hour of their services. Jack pushed them off, going into the run-down shops and taverns that lined Lycher Street. The stench of this part of London had Jack gasping for breath as he continued to search for Nora. He'd stop in one more tavern before he'd have to head back to his apartment for the night. He knew he risked being robbed, or worse, if he stayed on Lycher Street when it was dark.

He walked into the tavern, his eyes trying to adjust to the dimly lit building. It smelled like body odour, cigarettes, and bad whiskey. Jack choked back the urge to vomit as he searched the tavern. Nora. Was it really her?

A woman was desperately trying to fend off the groping advances of a large man, who was refusing to let go of the woman's arm.

Even as she raised a leg to kick him, he didn't flinch.

"Let me go, NOW!"

Jack recognised that voice. It WAS Nora. Without hesitating, Jack barrelled into the other man, punching him repeatedly until he let go of Nora. But the man wasn't about to give up. After several overturned tables and spilled mugs of ale from the fight, the tavern owner, Mr Johnson, angrily confronted Nora for causing trouble, telling her she no longer had a job there.

Stunned, Nora turned to face the man who had protected her. "Thank you." She couldn't look at him. She had to get her bag and leave. And face nights out on the streets again. She was too tired to even beg for her job. She would go. She had no fight left in her anymore.

"Wait! Nora?" A hand grabbed her arm.

"Let go of me you…" *But this man knows my name. Do I know him?*

She lifted her eyes to look at the man's face. "Jack? Is it really you?"

"Nora, it is you."

"Now go get your bag and get out of here Missy. You cost me a lot of money tonight. Now GO!"

"I'm coming with you," Jack said as Nora started to walk away, following her up the narrow stairs to the attic.

"Is…is this where you've been living, Nora?" Jack was shocked. And sick. Look what his father had done to her!

"Yes, I know it looks horrid, but it's safe up here. I'm not on the streets anymore."

It only took her a few minutes to pack her bag. "How did you find me, Jack? I never thought I'd see you again."

"I'd have searched the ends of the earth for you, Nora. It's okay. I'm so sorry for what my father did to you. He told me the whole horrid story, and the lie he'd made up about you stealing money. He was angry at me for standing up to him and telling him that I was going to marry you, no matter what he said. When he saw that he couldn't hurt me any longer, he decided to do the next best thing; the thing that he knew would hurt me the most. And that would be turning you out onto the streets. I don't see how I will ever forgive him for this."

Nora took his hand. "It's not your fault, Jack, I never blamed you. I blamed myself. I thought if I hadn't told you how I felt, you wouldn't have talked to your father, and I wouldn't have ended up here."

"It was never your fault, Nora. My father actually apologised to me for what he'd done to you. But he'll never have my forgiveness. You're safe now, Nora. I'll protect you and take care of you for the rest of my life. You'll never have to be scared again."

Nora insisted that it wouldn't be proper for her to stay in his apartment since they weren't married but Jack insisted that there was nowhere else he would take her. Now that he'd found her, he wasn't letting her go again.

Shyly agreeing, with assurance from Jack that she could sleep in the bed while he slept on the floor, Nora was overjoyed to see Jack again, although she felt ashamed of the circumstances that Jack had seen her in. What must he think of her working in a tavern with men groping her all the time? She hoped he didn't think less of her as she'd had no other choice.

After taking a long bath, Nora changed out of her uniform and put on the only clothes she had left in her bag – a blue pair of pants and a white shirt. She saw the earrings that Jack had given her for Christmas years ago and put them in her ears. It had been years since she'd worn them, too afraid that someone would steal them from her, but tonight was the perfect time to wear them.

"Nora, you look beautiful. You don't know how panicked I was, Nora. I worried that something terrible had happened to you. But I promised myself, and Sally, that I'd find you, no matter how long it took or how far I had to search."

Nora walked over to sit by his side.

"The earrings… you still have them…"

"Of course I do, Jack. You gave them to me; I'll never part with them. I love them."

Over the next two days, Nora opened up to Jack, telling him about the months she lived on the streets and in the rat infested building. She told him how she was turned down for work, even at the workhouse, until she'd run from the two men who tried to kidnap her and ended up in the tavern.

While it was hard for Jack to hear, Nora assured him that through it all, she had been okay. Yes, she was scared and lonely but she'd made it through. And that was all that mattered. She told Jack that his father had acted out of anger and had given no thought as to what awaited Nora on the streets, because his father had never been cast out on the streets. He'd had no idea that Nora wouldn't be able to find a job or a safe place to live. And while she understood why Jack was angry at his father, she insisted that he needed to forgive him, as that was the only family Jack had.

"Do you know what I would give to be able to talk to my mother and father again,

Jack? I'd give anything. And while you still have your father, I'm begging you, please talk to him. Make things right before it's too late. I've forgiven him, Jack, you need to too."

"In time, Nora, perhaps in time I will. But not right now. I hope you understand. He put your life in danger, and while you've forgiven him, I can't right now."

Nora nodded. She understood and knew Jack would reach out to his father once his anger and fear at losing Nora subsided.

"Nora?"

"Yes?"

"I love you. It's so good to be able to say that to you. I love you. I will forever, I promise you that."

"I love you, too. That's never changed."

"And you still want to marry me?"

"Of course! Did you think that would have changed?"

"I hoped not. I know it's later than we talked about, but how would you like to start planning our wedding? Whatever you want, you'll get. Cost is not an option, Nora, I want you to have the perfect day. A day that you will never forget."

"Do you want your father there?"

"Oh, he'll be there. Or his money will anyway. I'll make sure of that. If my Father still refuses to accept you as my wife, Nora, then he will not be a part of our lives. I will forgive him but he will not be welcome in our home."

That night as she said her prayers, Nora prayed that father and son would be able to reconcile. And if not, she would be a good wife to Jack, and a good mother to their children. They'd live a happy life together, and Sally would be by her side.

The next morning while Nora was still sleeping, Jack went back to his home to tell Sally that he'd found Nora. Crying tears of happiness, she wrapped her arms around Jack. "I don't know how I can ever thank you, Jack. Can I see her? Soon?"

"Yes, of course. You can come with me now. I've already informed Mrs Emsworth, and she's given you the rest of the day off."

"Nora! Nora, you're safe! I've missed you so much." Sally ran over to Nora, almost knocking her down as she wrapped her arms around her. "You can't ever do that again, Nora, I was so scared when I didn't hear from you in months. I thought something had happened to you."

"It's okay, Sally. I'm fine, thanks to Jack. I'm good, really. It was a rough couple of months but I survived. I promised you I'd see you again, and you know I'd never break my word to you."

"Tell her!" Jack couldn't keep the smile off of his face.'

Sally looked expectantly at Nora. "What? What is it?"

"We're getting married. As soon as we can."

"That's wonderful, Nora!"

"And, I wanted to wait until Sally was here…" Jack got down on one knee, pulling a small box out of his pants pocket. "Nora, will you do me the honour of being my wife?"

"Yes! Yes!"

"Sally, I expect you to help Nora plan the wedding," Jack said. "That's one of the reasons I brought you here."

"I would be honoured. Oh, Nora, I'm so happy for you. I knew this day would come, I just knew it."

Sally looked at Jack. "I told her from the beginning that you loved her, Jack, but she didn't believe me. I saw it in your face, just like I saw the love in Nora's face for you."

"Sally!" Nora blushed. "Now help me plan my wedding!"

Epilogue

Jack insisted on the two sisters having new dresses made up for the occasion. The girls had never owned dresses as elegant as those. One month after Jack's proposal, Nora and Jack were married.

"You look more beautiful than ever," Jack said, as his bride approached him at the altar.

"And you are more handsome than ever."

After the ceremony, Nora and Jack held hands, greeting the small gathering of guests that had come to the ceremony.

"Congratulations, Jack and Nora," Della and Lucy chimed in together. "You are such a beautiful bride, Nora."

Mrs Emsworth offered her congratulations, hugging both Jack and Nora.

"Is my father here?"

Mrs Emsworth shook her head. "I'm sorry, Jack. I spoke to him about it and told him he'd regret it if he didn't attend, but he refused."

Jack looked at Nora, and she saw the sadness in his eyes. Like Mrs Emsworth, she felt his father would regret this decision, even years down the road. But Mr Bradley could be a stubborn man, even in regards to his own son's wedding. But she still held out hope that, someday, there might be a reconciliation between father and son.

Life was good for Jack and Nora after their marriage. Nora loved the townhouse that Jack had rented to start their married lives in. Nora enjoyed decorating their home and feeling at peace in her life. It was a peace that she'd not felt since her parents had passed. She felt safe and secure. She felt loved and protected.

And one month after they had gotten married, Jack brought Sally over, a huge grin on his face.

"Hi, Sally. Did Jack bring you over for dinner?"

"Well, you can kind of say that, Nora." Sally looked at Jack.

"All right, what are you two up to?" Nora looked from Sally to Jack, and back at Sally again.

"I'm not just here for dinner. I'm here to stay!"

"What?!"

"Surprise!" Jack walked over to kiss his wife on her cheek. "I promised you I'd take care of you and Sally. Sally is going to be living with us. There's plenty of room…"

"Thank you! Have I told you that you are the best husband…"

"Yes, but I never get tired of hearing it," Jack teased her.

"Sally! I'm so happy. What more could I ever want? I have the loves of my life by my side. I can't get more blessed than this."

***

"Happy one year anniversary; I love you." Jack planted a kiss on his wife's forehead.

"Can you believe it's been one year, Jack! And, ouch, oooohh…"

"Nora, are you okay? Do you need to sit down?"

Nora laughed. "I'm fine. It's just the baby kicking again. The doctor said it could be anytime now."

"I hope it's today," Sally chimed in. "I can't wait to become an auntie."

"I think it will be today," Nora said as she put her hands on her stomach. "In fact, I think it'll be soon…"

Baby Luke arrived six hours later. Jack refused to rest, taking turns with Sally in caring for the new-born infant while Nora rested.

As baby Luke turned one month old, Nora insisted that Jack go see his father. "He doesn't know about Luke, Jack. Don't you think he has the right to know about his grandchild?"

It took Jack two more weeks, but he returned to his father's home, finally ready to make amends. It had taken him an entire year but he'd finally forgiven his father.

While Mr Bradley was surprised to see him, he was delighted to hear that Jack was now a father. Jack provided his father his address, telling him he was welcome anytime to see Luke.

It was four days later when a knock on the door startled Jack, Nora, and Sally.

"I'll get it," Sally said.

A few moments later, Sally walked back into the kitchen, followed by Mr Bradley.

A shocked Nora could only say hello.

Jack walked over to his father and shook his hand. "Welcome, Father. I have someone for you to meet."

As Mr Bradley held Luke, Nora could see the love the man had for his first grandchild. She could also see the love Jack had as he looked at his father holding his son.

When baby Luke was put to bed and Sally had excused herself, Mr Bradley apologised to Nora and Luke. For everything that had happened. He told them he couldn't take back the mistakes he'd made in the past, and that he would never repeat those same mistakes in the future. He'd missed his son and didn't want to miss out on his grandson growing up. He welcomed Nora as his son's wife and gave his blessing for their marriage, even though it was over a year too late.

And he promised to come around more as he left.

"We talked about me coming back into the business with him. I think I'm ready for that now. I let him know that I'll be happy to take over the business when he feels it's time for him to retire."

"That sounds like the perfect plan, Jack."

"All right, Stanley should be here any minute." Sally walked over to the door. "I'll be back soon."

"We'll be waiting," Jack teased. Nora and Jack both liked Stanley, who worked as a clerk in one of the local shops. They'd been courting for three months, and Nora saw a wedding in their future.

"We are finally alone," Nora smiled at Jack. "How did we get so lucky, Jack? To have such perfect lives?"

"It's because of love. Love makes everything right with the world."

And their daughter, born two years later, would have agreed with her parents.

Printed in Great Britain
by Amazon